An International Mountie

Adventures of the First Woman Mountie. Book 4

LAURIE SCHRAMM

This book is a work of historical fiction, set in the 1970s. Although most of the historical references are accurate, a few are not, and names, characters, places, and incidents are either the product of the author's imagination or are used fictitiously. Any resemblance to actual persons, living or dead is entirely coincidental.

Print ISBN: 978-1-9994940-6-3
ePub ISBN: 978-1-9994940-7-0

Laurie Schramm

Miners and packers ascending the summit of the Chilkoot Pass in the winter of 1898. Photo by E.A. Hegg, courtesy of Library and Archives Canada, C-005142.

Laurie Schramm

DEDICATION

To Max

Laurie Schramm

CONTENTS

Laurie Schramm

ACKNOWLEDGMENTS

Many thanks to my supportive readers, C/Supt. William Schramm (Ret.) who also kindly allowed my main character to borrow his Regimental Number, Ann Marie, Katherine, Moira, and Jayme for their comments and suggestions on drafts of this book.

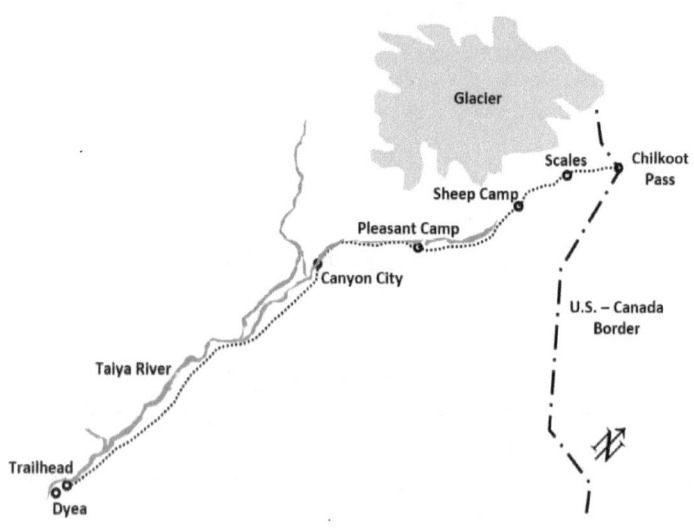

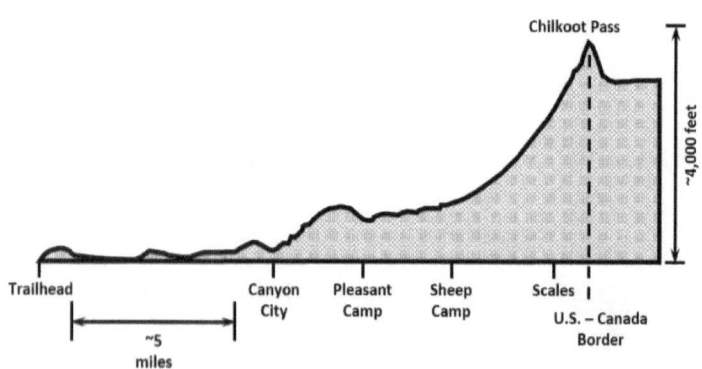

LIST OF CHARACTERS
(IN ORDER OF APPEARANCE)

- Inspector Stone, NWMP
- Corporal Frank Pool, NWMP
- Lucy Lake, a Girl Guide Pathfinder
- Allison Smith, a Girl Guide Pathfinder. Lucy's best friend
- Max, an orange Mackerel Tabby Cat
- Constable Alexandra (Alex) Houston, RCMP
- Assistant Commissioner George MacLeod, RCMP Security Service
- Silver, an Alaskan Malamute. Alex's friend and companion
- Ross and Sally Peake, Owner/Operators of Alaskan Malamute Adventures, Dyea, AK.
- Goldie, an Alaskan Malamute. Silver's sister
- King and Queenie, Alaskan Malamutes. Silver's parents
- Norm Poole, Hunting and Fishing Guide
- Jim Dumont, Hunting and Fishing Guide
- George Carter, Chief of Police, Skagway, AK
- Staff Sergeant Robert (Bob) G. Simpson, RCMP Security Service
- Mark Johnston, Search and Rescue Coordinator, Skagway, AK
- Julie Sawyer, Seasonal Park Ranger, Klondike Gold Rush National Historic Park, AK
- Captain Donald (Don) Harrison, Military Intelligence, Canadian Forces

1 PRELUDE: THE CHILKOOT

April 12, 1898
Chilkoot Trail, Alaska,
Two miles north of the Canyon City camp.

Sitting in the snow, huddled-up against a tree trunk, bleeding, and nearing complete exhaustion Corporal Frank Pool, of the North West Mounted Police[1], knew he was in trouble. He had faced danger many times in his first year of being posted to the Klondike but now, for the first time, he had to face the practical reality that he might not survive the day.

It had, at first, seemed like just another day when Superintendent Sam Steele[2] had assigned Inspector Stone, Frank, and five constables to transport some 150,000 dollars in gold and notes over the Chilkoot Pass, down the mountain to Skagway, Alaska, and from there on to Victoria, British Columbia. The gold had been collected as customs duties, mining lease registrations, and production royalties from miners and others that had joined the Klondike Gold Rush.

The gold rush had been triggered by the discovery, nineteen months earlier (in August, 1896), of placer gold at Bonanza Creek, which is a tributary of the Klondike River. As the news permeated North America, and then the rest of the world, the Klondike became – almost overnight – the scene of the greatest gold rush in North American history. It began with prospectors, but then spread to anyone willing to

1

travel and risk their lives in the pursuit of potentially striking it rich, whether by mining, providing services to the miners, or simply stealing from the miners. Determined to keep the peace, at least on the Canadian side of the border, Mounted Police reinforcements and supplies were almost immediately sent into the Yukon to bolster the small detachment that had already been in place.

Now, with the long 1897/98 winter finally beginning to retreat, it was time to begin escorting batches of gold ingots out of the territory. Although it was considered 'safe' to transport valuables on the Canadian side of the border, the same could not be said of travel on the American side, which had already fully earned the reputation of being a completely lawless part of the "Wild, Wild West." The portion of Alaska stretching from Skagway to the summit of the Chilkoot Pass, in particular, had become controlled in its entirety by the infamous Soapy Smith[3] and his huge gang of thieves and accomplices.

The Mounties' main concern was not for the rigors of the trail, the mud and snow, the likelihood of avalanches and premature river-ice breakup, or the virtual certainty of bad weather along the way, but rather how to get the gold past Soapy and his gang.

Soapy had so many spies and accomplices that the maintenance of secrecy was viewed as sheer fantasy. Instead, Superintendent Steele and Inspector Stone had quietly let it be known that Stone was being transferred to the prairies, specifically Regina, and was taking with him only his baggage. The men, in turn, each carried on their horses one large box or trunk, plus their ordinary Mounted Police kit bag. The boxes and trunks were empty — simply part of the illusion. The gold ingots were hidden in the kit bags beneath layers of clothing and pemmican[4].

As the group set out, there was no immediate danger from Soapy Smith or his gang. Steele and his Mounties had done such a good job of enforcing peace on the Canadian side that it was rare indeed that any member of Soapy's gang crossed the border to test the Mounties' mettle. So, it was natural for Stone's patrol to expect a quiet journey to the summit of Chilkoot Pass. Trouble, if there was to be trouble, was expected on their descent from the summit on the American side, particularly as they descended the steepest section that led to The Scales, during which they could be simultaneously assailed by rough terrain, bad weather, and well-hidden attackers. If they were going to be ambushed, they thought, that is where they would have to have their wits about them. This was a very reasonable, and time-tested, rationale.

Unfortunately, they were only partly right.

The first sixteen and a half miles of their journey were completely uneventful. On the first day, they proceeded from their headquarters at Lake Bennett, past Lindemann City, and then above the tree-line to Happy Camp, where they spent the night. The second day, they proceeded past Stone Crib and up the short but steep section to the summit of the Chilkoot Pass. Here the Mounties had a permanent camp and Customs Post that was equipped with men, provisions, two Maxim machine guns, and ammunition. At this exposed but secure post they paused for a rest, and to ensure that their water bottles were full, before embarking on the great descent that was to come.

The next phase of their journey was to carefully descend some 3,500 feet, of which the first section – from the summit to The Scales – was the steepest, involving the descent of a thousand feet in just over half of a mile. This was arduous going, as the entire slope was still covered in snow and, although there was a well-travelled path, the men had to proceed on foot, each leading their horse behind him.

Experienced mountaineers know well that, regardless of whether one is ascending or descending a mountain, there is a psychological tendency to relax at the end of a strenuous and/or hazardous segment. None of the Mounties were particularly experienced at mountaineering, so they may not have been aware of this, and whether such was part of Soapy's calculations or not will probably never be known. When the Mounties had reached The Scales, Inspector Stone gave a huge sigh of relief and allowed his men to take a break to rest and relax, after which they resumed their downward travel. When they reached Sheep Camp, and had put most of the steep decline behind them, the Inspector let out an even greater sigh of relief and ordered his men to remount their horses. They should now be able to relax somewhat, he thought, as they rode the much gentler terrain for the rest of the way.

The ambush came two miles further ahead, as the Mounties were passing Pleasant Camp and riding up a short rise on the west side of the valley. It was here that Soapy Smith and his gang had positioned themselves. Soapy had brought twenty of his men, every one of them armed with pistols and some of them carrying repeating rifles. Here, they had hidden themselves. The location was well chosen. In addition to having the element of surprise, they were below the tree-line at this point, so Soapy and his men were able to take cover among the plentiful supply of trees and dull grey boulders. From their hiding places, when the time came, and completely without warning, they suddenly unleashed a blistering volley of gunfire.

Although caught completely off-guard, the Mounties were quick enough to respond. At the first sounds of shots Inspector Stone had ordered his men to dismount, spread out, take cover, and return fire. There was no need for any of these orders, however, as to a man they had immediately leapt from their horses and spread out. Having established what cover they could, each Mountie returned fire on their own.

Although outnumbered four-to-one, and with hastily chosen cover, the Mounties soon gained the advantage in the gun battle that ensued. This was because, although Soapy and his men had chosen their location and their cover with care, their shooting was both undisciplined and generally poorly aimed. The Mounties, on the other hand were well-trained, disciplined, and much better shots. They took their time, conserved their ammunition, and carefully squeezed off their shots only at the most favourable, if fleeting, exposures of Soapy's men. As a result, after what seemed like an eternity but was in fact only about fifteen minutes, more than half of Soapy's men's guns had been silenced, whether because their owners had become incapacitated or killed, or because they had rashly expended their ammunition and were no longer able to participate in the ambush.

At this point in the battle only about half of Soapy's men were still firing, but the survivors had learned their lesson. They were now conserving their remaining ammunition, and were finally choosing their shots with greater care – although their accuracy had not noticeably improved.

Correctly guessing that these were the more skilled and experienced members of Soapy's gang, and not wanting to press the providential luck that had so far enabled all of his men to avoid being shot, Stone made the difficult decision to order his men to run for their horses.

Here was another difference between these opposing forces. Whereas Soapy and his men had ridden whatever horses they could conveniently borrow or steal in Skagway, all Mountie horses had been chosen with *great care and carefully trained to stand fast under fire. As a result, every one of them was to be found patiently standing nearby, waiting for their human masters and partners. Had Soapy been a better strategist he would have had his men shoot the horses first, thus effectively trapping his quarry where they had taken cover. Perhaps he had thought it unnecessary. Amazingly, however, none of the Mounties' horses had yet been injured – or worse – in the gun battle.*

As the Mounties ran for their horses, Stone yelled out his orders to disperse and "make a run for it as best they could" straight down the trail, through the centre of Soapy and his men, and on to Finnegan's Point, where they would regroup.

Stone was taking a dangerous, calculated risk with this manoeuvre but he judged it to be less risky than remaining in place with declining ammunition and against a superior, if diminished, force.

For the most part his plan was successful.

Seeing the Mounties break from cover and run for their horses, Soapy and the remainder of his men immediately knew that their targets were about to "make a run for it," and they all stood up in plain sight and attempted to shoot the fleeing Mounties, and/or their horses before they could escape.

Fortunately for the Mounties, their zig-zag run for their horses coupled with the gang's lack of coordination and poor marksmanship soon took them right through Soapy and his men. Up the rest of the hill they raced, quickly moving beyond the range of the pistols, and leaving only the few attackers that were equipped with repeating rifles to worry about. Soon, however, they gained the crest of the hill, and disappeared over the other side, taking them out of sight of the rifles as well.

Unfortunately for Frank, who was the last to reach his horse, two of the repeating rifles had been aimed at him throughout the final phase of the battle. For his part, he'd quickly mounted his horse and spurred him ahead, but no sooner had he passed the gang than one bullet hit him and another struck his horse.

Frank had immediately fallen from his saddle, but his horse stood firm. Reaching up for his saddle and reins, he was just barely able to remount. Then, leaning far forward over his saddle horn, he urged his horse forward, and they managed to slowly ride off in the direction of their comrades, who were already over the crest of the hill and far ahead along the trail, well out of sight.

Left behind were Soapy Smith and ten very angry and vocal gang members, several of whom continued to fire in the direction of the escaping Mounties notwithstanding the fact that there was no longer anyone in sight at whom to actually aim. Although none of the gang were motivated to jump on their horses in pursuit, their continued shooting had the unfortunate effect of convincing the fleeing Mounties that they were being actively pursued. As a result, they continued their retreat without taking time to assess whether or not all of their detail was still intact.

For his part, Frank didn't feel very intact. It was all he could do to hang on and remain in the saddle. As a result, he made it most of the way down the hill towards Canyon City before he realized that, like him, his horse Angel had been shot. He'd been so concerned with staying on the trail and stemming his bleeding wound that he didn't even notice the first few times that Angel had stumbled, but eventually it became clear that something was wrong. Quickly dismounting to check, he noticed two things simultaneously. One was that there was a long trail of blood behind him; and the other was that Angel was trembling violently. He no sooner found the entrance wound and began an attempt to stop the bleeding than Angel raised his head, gave out a huge sigh, collapsed, and died. Brave and loyal to the end, Mounted Police Horse Angel had lived up to his name and given everything he'd had to get his master away from the gun battle.

Mentally attempting to set aside mourning for a more appropriate time, Frank removed the saddle, placed the horse blanket over Angel's head, and whispered a few words of thanks and good-bye. Then he wearily grabbed his kit bag, forced himself to stand, and trudged ahead on foot.

As Frank determinedly kept moving forward, it wasn't long before pain, loss of blood, and the encroaching cold began to take their toll. Frank eventually fell into a kind of delirium that caused him to lose the proper trail and follow a game trail that branched off to the west, thus missing the canyon, and Canyon City, completely.

Most of the snow had melted away at this elevation so that a mile along the game trail, Frank encountered a creek. Mistaking this for the

Taiya River, rather than one of its tributaries, he followed it further west. Four miles later the creek abruptly ended, and while trying to understand what had happened, Frank collapsed at the base of a youngish balsam fir tree. He was now cold, exhausted, still bleeding, disoriented, and completely lost. Realizing that his chances of survival were now running very low, Frank forced himself to eat a few bites of his pemmican, then used his sheath knife to scrape a shallow depression in the ground near the base of the tree. He placed his kit bag into the depression and covered it with the earth that he'd removed. On top of this, he built a broad but low cairn of rocks to mark the spot.

With his load lightened, he struggled to his feet and staggered back the way he had come, retracing his steps in hopes of regaining the proper trail back to his post. It was impossible to lose his way back because of the bright red trail of blood, but stamina was another matter. Sheer determination was all that kept him moving at this point and, amazingly, he managed three of the miles back, but only three.

Corporal Frank Pool of the North West Mounted Police collapsed and died where his searching colleagues later found him, just two miles west of the Chilkoot Trail, and slightly north of Canyon City. Although they searched until dusk made further searching impossible, they never found the buried kit bag.

Laurie Schramm

2 ALASKA BOUND

My name is Alexandra Houston. My friends call me Alex.

In the summer of 1974, I'd been 24 years old, and feeling like my career was at a standstill. I'd studied chemistry at university and liked it, but not enough to pursue science as a career. I'd reset my sights on police work next, and had joined the Metropolitan Toronto Police force (Metro). Although policing seemed like a better fit for me than science, my two years with Metro had mostly comprised routine administrative- and traffic duties. These assignments were important, and needed to be done by somebody, and done well. But for me, they didn't fit the Hollywood vision of policing that I had developed, and I hadn't found them to be very challenging.

They say you should be careful what you wish for.

My life soon changed drastically, beginning with an unexpected meeting. Without explanation, my Captain had sent me to go and see a Royal Canadian Mounted Police (RCMP) officer that wanted to meet me. My reaction to this was apprehension, and I wondered what I could possibly have messed-up so badly that it had caught the notice of our national police force.

That's how I first came to meet Assistant Commissioner George MacLeod. After a lengthy conversation that I belatedly realized was an interview, he told me that he had asked my Captain (his friend) to recommend one of his young officers for a special pilot project he had in mind. He wanted someone who wanted to accomplish things, someone eager and tenacious, someone chomping at the bit to be allowed to do some 'real' police work, and... someone female. At this point he had shed his stern 'Mountie look,' relaxed his entire body, chuckled, and said that my Captain had recommended the "biggest pain in the butt" in his Division - me.

Assistant Commissioner MacLeod had explained that the 'Force' had fallen behind the times, and that its senior leadership wanted to build a more diverse police force. "We're going to be recruiting immigrants, visible minorities, maybe even people with some kinds of disabilities as well," he said, "But we have to start somewhere, and that somewhere is by engaging women." He wanted to try a first 'pilot test' with a woman, but that pilot test had to succeed as it would pave the way for an entire first troop of policewomen that would follow. He had thought of using someone that had already qualified as a policewoman, and simply re-train them in the 'RCMP way.'

That had brought me up to full attention. "Wait a minute! Do basic training all over again?"

"Yes!" he'd replied, "that's the only way you can possibly succeed. In the old days of the Northwest Mounted Police, a person could get appointed straight into the Force, even as a commissioned officer, if they had the right political connections. No more. Now everyone starts out the same way, as a Constable, and by going through the same basic training. If you want to have any hope of being accepted, much less respected, that's how you have to begin."

So, in the fall of 1974, I went through training at the RCMP's 'Depot' Division training centre in Regina, dealt with the good and the bad issues that came with being the first woman to train there, and survived to become the first woman Mountie. I hadn't intended for it to happen, really.

The opportunity just came and found me.

After training, or re-training if you like, I'd been posted to Radium City, a small town in very northern Saskatchewan that, in its early days, had been a great uranium mining centre. Although my new boss, Corporal Morrison, had told me that nothing interesting ever happened around there, he'd been wrong, and I'd had to rescue him from a mine collapse, run our entire detachment single-handed while he was confined to hospital for six weeks, get rescued by a strange dog from near-death, solve a mystery, and find and catch a murderer – all in only four months!

The dog was named Silver. Investigating a mysterious series of break-ins had led me to some unusual places, including several abandoned uranium mines. In one such mine I'd fallen through a trap and found myself hanging precariously over the sharp edge of a vertical mine shaft. Unable to get out and tiring fast, I was saved by the almost magical appearance of what I first took to be a wolf, which gave me quite a scare, but turned out to be Silver, an Alaskan Malamute. Silver somehow sensed that I was in danger, had decided to help, and with his assistance I had been able to climb up and out of the raise. To make a long story short[5], while I'd continued to investigate the case, he had attached himself to me, was eventually given to me, and we'd been close friends ever since.

Sometime later I'd found myself in another surprise meeting with the same Assistant Commissioner MacLeod. Once again, a "coffee meeting" had turned into an interview and, once again, he had something new in mind for me. By this time, he'd become head of the Force's Security Service[6] and, unsurprisingly, he had some new ideas he wanted to try out by way of some experimental pilot projects. One of them involved me.

That had taken me to Ottawa in November of 1975, where I joined the Security Service. My new boss, Staff Sergeant Robert ("Call me Bob") G. Simpson, introduced me to the shady worlds of spies, counter-espionage, anarchists, and terrorists, and then sent Silver and I to Northern Alberta, undercover, to help look into a series of bomb threats directed at oil sands companies.

Our path to the oil sands was indirect, however, as Silver and I were first sent to Innisfail, Alberta, to be trained as a police dog and handler team. "If that dog is going to go everywhere with you, then we should get him trained too," I'd been told. Both Bob and Assistant Commissioner MacLeod had been interested in, and seemingly amused by, the undercover possibilities presented by the first female Mountie and her canine partner. So in that way, Silver had officially joined the Mounties too and we were sent to Fort McMurray, undercover to investigate the bomb threats. Our cover stories had held up just long enough for us to identify and apprehend the bomber, although not before a few more adventures. In one of those adventures I'd been able to save Silver's life, which evened up the score and reinforced the feeling I'd long had that our destinies were inter-twined. That had been 1976.

In the Spring of 1977, Silver and I were sent, undercover again, to Nova Scotia to look into a mysterious weather station on Cape Breton Island. This had involved a lot of SCUBA diving, which was a lot of fun, and a peek inside the shadowy world of international espionage, which had at times been downright terrifying. By the end of July, the case had been wrapped-up, and Silver and I had been ordered to go off on vacation and get some rest.

Through our adventures together I'd often wondered about Silver's origins, particularly since he was such an unusual dog. So, with the gift of free time, I decided to go explore Silver's past. *That should be restful*, I had thought.

I was wrong.

***

August, 1977

Having put things in order back in Ottawa, Silver and I drove west and made brief stops in Saskatchewan and Alberta to visit with colleague-friends along the way. That part alone saw us drive over 2,150 miles in five days.

It was so great to be back out west again! Most people just see the flat prairie that characterizes south-central Saskatchewan, without realizing that there is a huge proliferation of gorgeous lakes in the northern half of the province. Alberta, of course has the grandeur of the Rocky Mountains.

Our Alaska adventure began in earnest when we left Edmonton for the drive to Skagway, which involved driving another 1,300 miles. That drive was more fun for me because it was all new. Driving northwest from Edmonton took us through a lot of sparsely populated, wide open spaces. Two days' driving took us well past Fort Saint John and Fort Nelson, to an oasis at Liard River. This was a hot oasis, as Liard River's claim to fame is a large natural hot spring beautifully positioned in boreal forest.

I'd had no idea that the hot springs even existed, but once we got there, I immediately decided that it was an ideal spot for a break and stayed there for the night and all the next morning. The most memorable part for me was the morning soak in the springs when the entire area was covered in a low fog bank, and the fact that the springs had been developed into two huge pools connected by a modest waterfall. One pool was formed by the source water flowing up from underground, so it was very hot! The second pool was cooler, so you could practically pick your desired water temperature by moving around in the pools. It also turned out that you could swim underneath the waterfall, come up behind it, and sit there with rock behind you and a solid curtain of hot water falling right in front of you. It was a natural steam chamber. It was gorgeous, and it was very relaxing.

Silver, with his natural aversion to water had, of course, refused to enter the hot spring and simply watched my antics from a safe distance, while managing to project an attitude of amused tolerance.

Departing from Liard River, we were well along the famous Alaska Highway route. It was exciting to drive a highway that I'd heard and read so much about, although I was a bit concerned about all the stories of rough road patches and the hazards to vehicles. Bearing those stories in mind, I hoped that being in a four-wheel-drive truck, with good ground clearance, would enable us to make the trip without serious mishaps.

It turned out that the highway wasn't as bad as I feared, although it did call for cautious driving. This was brought

home to me by a chance meeting with a fellow traveler, in the coffee shop of a roadside gas station. He had been travelling in the opposite direction, driving a medium-sized RV and told me that he had hit a 'rough patch' that left him with a broken axle. His RV had been towed to the gas station and he had already been waiting for a week for the garage to get the parts they needed to fix it! His hard-won advice to me was to pay close attention to the changing road conditions, and to drive slowly. Taking his advice, and with a more rugged vehicle, I had no real problems with the highway.

An afternoon's drive took us over the border into the Yukon Territory and Watson Lake. Following an overnight stay there, an easy day's driving took us further northwest through changing terrain and scenery until we reached Whitehorse. On day 5, we had an early morning look around Whitehorse, where I paid a quick visit to the RCMP Detachment and borrowed a locker in which to deposit my gun. After that, we back-tracked a bit, and then drove more or less due west, up and over the mountains, across the border and into the United States. We made it down the mountains to Skagway by mid-day.

***

All I knew about Silver's background was that he had been born and raised in Skagway, Alaska, and that he had been sold to Norm Poole, a Radium City hunting and fishing guide, for his dogsled team. This had apparently worked out so well that, at some point, Silver had become Norm's lead dog.

Although Silver had attached himself to me[5] shortly before he (Norm) had died, under the terms of Norm's will his legal ownership had passed to Ruby Gillespie, the owner/manager of Radium City's Coffee Shop. Fortunately, before I was transferred out to another assignment, Ruby had kindly transferred Silver's ownership to me. Ruby had even found the original bill of sale in Norm's files, so I knew the name and address of the Skagway sled-dog breeders. Their place turned out to be just West of Skagway – across the Skagway River and along the route to the neighbouring ghost-town of Dyea. The town had hosted a busy port during the Klondike Gold Rush, but it was eventually overtaken by the deeper water port of Skagway, and the final straw for Dyea had come when Skagway became the terminus for the White Pass and Yukon Route Railroad (which had decided to follow the White Pass Trail rather than the Chilkoot Trail for its ascent up the mountain and to the Yukon).

Now, nearly 80 years later, my travel guide explained that only a few people still lived on small homesteads in the valley near Dyea. Apparently, the main local tourist attraction was the late-summer salmon-spawning run, which attracted bears (black bears and brown bears) and eagles. After a few false turns, we were able to find *Alaskan Malamute Adventures*, the

Ross Peake

homestead of Ross Peake, who had been listed as Silver's breeder and seller.

As we turned into the yard, we were greeted by Ross himself, who was a bit frightening at first glance. He had rather wild-looking, longish grey hair, and a very full grey and white beard, but friendly and incredibly clear, penetrating eyes. Those eyes didn't miss much: with only the briefest glance at me he took one look at my companion and yelled: "Silver!"

In the same instant, Silver had recognized and rushed up to him, stood straight up on his hind legs, with his forepaws on Ross' chest, his tail wagging, and proceeded to lick every part of Ross' face that he could get at – which was essentially all of it, although it was mostly beard.

I had stepped back to give Silver room, and was watching bemusedly as Ross peered through Silver's frantic licking to take a second look at me.

"Alex Houston," I said, by way of introduction. "I wanted to see where Silver grew up and it looks like we've found the right place."

"Well I'll say that you have. My name's Ross Peake, and any friend of Silver's is a friend of ours!"

"Ours?"

"My sister, Sally, and I run this place," Ross answered. "She's around somewhere. Why don't you come for a look around then, once we find Sally, we can all go inside for a chat?"

I readily agreed, and Ross showed Silver and I around the place.

The first thing that struck me was the huge yard full of dog houses. Each dog seemed to have their own house, which resembled a rectangular box on short legs. Raising the dog houses up on legs presumably provided an easy way to keep the dog houses warmer and drier than if they sat on the ground. Each dog house had an open, square door and a flat roof that projected out over the door. I had seen sled-dog houses like this in Radium City, Saskatchewan and I wondered whether the design may have originated here in

Alaska, or possibly in the Northern Canadian territories. Certainly, the dogs seemed to appreciate the flat roofs as many of them were sprawled on the tops of their dog houses, lounging and either looking lazily around or napping.

The second thing that struck me, was the apparent variety of breeds. "I had the impression that northern sled dogs were usually Siberian Huskies or Alaskan Malamutes," I said.

"That was true in the beginning," agreed Ross. "Alaskan Malamutes and Siberian Huskies are the traditional sled-dogs, going way back in history. They are well adapted to the cold, and they're strong enough to be able to pull heavy loads over great distances. When dog-sledding was the only practical way to get around, and when it was necessary for hunting, then the Alaskan Malamutes and Siberian Huskies were the breeds of choice. Nowadays though, most dog-sledding is for fun or sport, like the dog-sled races that are put on in different countries."

"Like the Iditarod[7]," I suggested.

"Exactly," said Ross, clearly pleased that I was familiar with the name. "That's the most famous dog-sled race in North America, but there are also some great races in the Yukon, and in the Scandinavian countries. In fact, some mushers take their teams all around the world."

"So now you just need speed?" I asked.

"It's not quite that simple. The dogs still need to be able to handle the cold, and they still need to have endurance, and there are a few other things too. For example, we look for dogs that are curious, friendly, flexible, and co-operative team-players."

"Just like picking people for human teams," I commented.

"Exactly," he said, again sounding pleased. "But for the competitive racers, speed has become a larger factor. Speed and gait."

"Gait?"

"Gait! The ability to run efficiently and consistently at different speeds, and the ability to switch smoothly from one speed to another – particularly in 'synch' with the rest of the team."

"Wow, it's a lot more complicated than I'd imagined."

"Things have certainly progressed," Ross agreed. "The winner of the first Iditarod took almost three weeks to reach Nome, but modern racers can do it in close to ten days – that's a big change! Anyway, the sled-dogs that have been specifically bred to produce all these qualities are called Alaskan Huskies. They're still descended from Siberian Huskies and Alaskan Malamutes, but with other breeds mixed-in as well."

"I'd never heard of Alaskan Huskies before," I commented.

"Well, Alaskan Huskies will probably never be recognized by the Kennel Club, but they're a real breed to the rest of us!"

"Are there any Alaskan Huskies here?"

"Sure. I'll introduce you to some a bit later. You can call us traditionalists, but we also still breed Siberian Huskies and Alaskan Malamutes – like Silver here," he said, reaching out to tussle Silver's fur. "Of course, Silver's grey-blue eyes are unusual among Alaskan Malamutes, and he'd be disqualified as a purebred, but we're not interested in 'show dogs' here."

"Do you race though?" I asked.

"Oh, we race alright. Each season we do the race here, and then some of the Klondike races too. The difference is that we race for fun, and to keep the old spirit alive. So, we don't need the fastest dogs, and we don't push ourselves or our dogs to the limits. It's a big tradition around here. We enjoy the people that come to watch and run the races… and, like I said, I guess we just race for fun and to maintain the spirit of the thing. After all," he laughed, "dog mushing is the Alaska State Sport!"

By this time, we had walked around the large kennel area and the just-as-large training area. Some of the dog runs and jumps reminded me a bit of the RCMP Dog Service Training Centre that Silver and I had trained at in Innisfail, Alberta. The next part of the compound comprised a couple of large Quonset-style huts. Ross explained that these buildings contained a workshop and storage area for dog sleds and summer sleds.

We were walking towards the Quonset huts when Silver suddenly lifted his head, took a big sniff, gave out a distinct "Yip," and darted ahead of us. After only running about five yards though, he suddenly came to an abrupt stop, at which point he lowered his shoulders, placed his two front legs out on the ground in front of him, and lowered his head to the ground in a very deliberate 'bow'. I had seen dogs do that as a signal of non-aggression and wanting to play with another dog, but I'd never seen Silver do it before.

No sooner had I taken in this strange behavior than I noticed that a reddish-gold-coloured dog had come out of one of the buildings and was running full-tilt towards Silver. Other than the colouring, this dog looked quite a lot like Silver, and I began to have some suspicions at that point. I wasn't able to get a close look at this new dog right away, because the meeting of the two dogs immediately turned into a kind of wrestling match in which their bodies twisted and turned in all directions, accompanied by a bunch of growling sounds that sounded fairly loud but happy. You might have to be a 'dog person' to appreciate this, but there's a distinct difference in tone between dogs' happy growling and their angry or defensive growling.

Ross immediately began to chuckle. "It warms the heart to see those two back together again," he said.

"I take it that they know each other?"

"I should say they do! They're brother and sister after all. Her name's Goldie. Let's give them a moment and then I'll call her over for introductions."

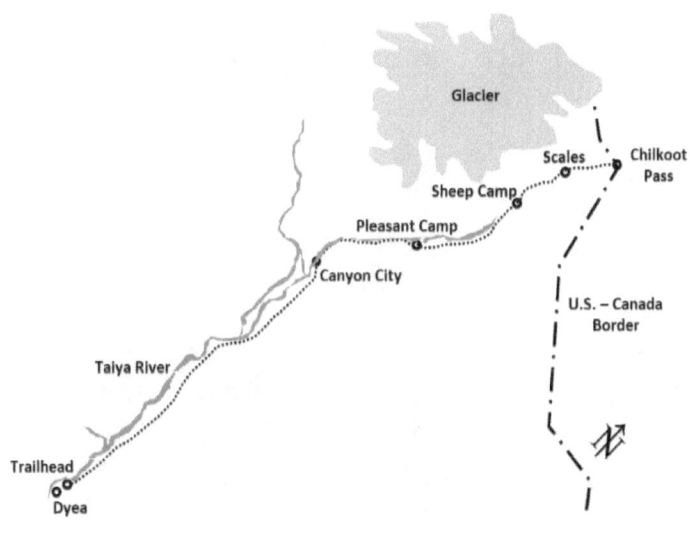

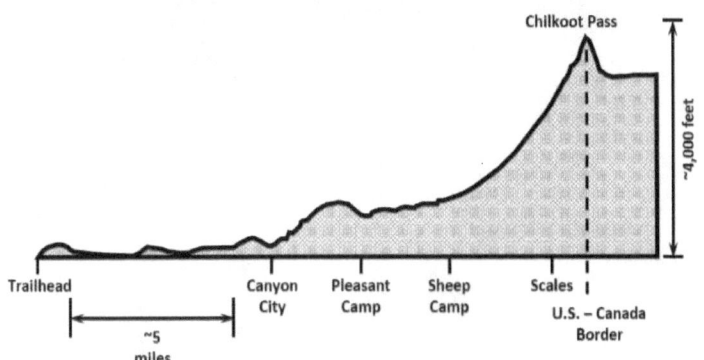

3 THE CHILKOOT REVISITED

August, 1977
Chilkoot Trail, Alaska,
Two miles north of the Canyon City camp.

It had all started out as such a grand, grown-up type adventure.

Lucy Lake was twelve years old. She had been part of the Canadian Girl Guides since starting out as a 'Brownie' at age seven[8]. As the years had gone by, she had been proud to graduate to 'Guides' the previous year (in 1976).

Something Lucy enjoyed about getting older was being able to do more interesting things, and one of the things the older Guides got to do was go on outdoor, or even international, trips. This trip had been both: a chance for her entire patrol to go to Skagway, Alaska and backpack the Chilkoot Trail all the way back to Canada. Back in 1897 and 1898, most of the prospectors and miners had made their way to Skagway, then to nearby Dyea, and from there had hiked and climbed the 17-mile trail to the summit, crossed into Canada, and then hiked another 16 miles to Lake Bennett. Lucy and her patrol were travelling that very same route.

On their first day Lucy, her five patrol-mates, and their two adult leaders had shouldered their heavy backpacks and started out from Dyea – just like the miners had done some 80 years earlier. Those early miners would have been amazed to see their patrol hiking along in their blue uniform shirts and shorts, wearing their traditional navy-blue berets, their bandanna-like ties (white, with red maple leaves and blue border), and their modern, aluminum-frame backpacks. The miners would have been even more impressed with the contents of those packs, which included lightweight freeze-dried foods and down sleeping bags.

The patrol felt a bit of the pain of the prospectors almost immediately as there was a quarter-mile section of the trail that felt like it was almost straight up. Between not having had a chance to really warm up on the hike and the burden of their heavy backpacks, it was hard going and soon had them all huffing and puffing. Their leaders assured them that this was like an initiation, and that the rest of the day would be much easier, but Lucy was in good company in thinking that maybe this hike wasn't such a great idea after all.

No one had wanted to be the one to give up, however, and after pausing to catch their breath the patrol had continued. The next seven miles of the trail to Canyon City had alternated up and down but had seemed quite easy in comparison with the initial stretch. As they hiked along beside the Taiya River they had marveled at the rugged beauty of their surroundings. Along each side of the river were scattered huge boulders and piles of sand and gravel, beyond that were groves of willow, poplar, and birch trees, and further out beyond that a range of steep and towering mountains. There were wild flowers growing here and there, among the rocks, squirrels running around and chattering in the trees, and even a few bald eagles sitting up high in the trees. Along the way they passed the ruins of an old sawmill, several shacks, and the odd bit of machinery rusting away.

As they passed Canyon City, the numbers of boulders lying about increased dramatically. These ranged in size from small to huge and, in many cases, they had one or more nearly-flat sides – indicating that they had been broken away from larger boulders rather than simply eroded down in size.

The forest started to change too. In some areas, a small number of brave-looking, individual trees raised their heads here and there among the rocks. Their leaders explained that these were survivors of avalanches and rockslides that had come racing down the mountainside sometime in the past. Some slopes were even more stark, with no tress on them at all. The leaders explained that, in these areas, frequent avalanches and rock slides had completely wiped out the trees and prevented new ones from growing. At the bottoms of the barren slopes were piled masses of rock interspersed with the remnants of shattered trees that had been uprooted and carried down with the rocks and/or snow. The most impressive thing, to some of the girls, was how huge some of the fractured tree trunks were!

Beyond Canyon City they'd crossed a suspension bridge and then passed more ruins of old cabins and other artifacts, like cooking utensils and even a large iron stove – all lying scattered about here and there, continuing to rust away as they had been for nearly eighty years. The sense of hiking in a virtual museum continued as they progressed, passing more artifacts and even long lengths of downed telegraph wire.

Although the air was cool, the weather had been good and the trail dry, so they'd had little difficulty making it to their planned first campsite at Mile 10: Pleasant Camp. After a long day of backpacking it had been a relief to ditch their packs, eat a hot supper, relax around their camp-stoves, and finally crawl into their tents for the night.

Lucy shared a tent with her best friend, Allison Smith. Once they were both safely inside, Lucy opened her pack and released her secret passenger: Max, a Mackerel Tabby cat. He had orange, tiger-striped short hair and a bob tail, making him look somewhat like a small, domesticated version of a wildcat. Despite his appearance, Max was actually very social and playful, and Lucy considered him to be her second-best friend. It was for this reason that she had smuggled Max into the Guides' trip by the simple expedient of hiding him in the top of her backpack.

Although he was an exceptionally patient cat, Max did have to be let out from time to time, of course. For this purpose, he had to wear a light harness to which Lucy could attach a thin but strong leash. With Allison's help Lucy had been able to be fairly discreet so far. Most of the other girls knew about Max, of course, and they considered him to be something in the nature of a trip mascot. Together, and unaware that they were acting foolishly, they had successfully concealed Max's presence from their adult patrol-leaders.

As the evening chill permeated their tent, Max prudently curled up inside Lucy's sleeping bag with his back nestled between the back of her head and the top of one shoulder. As Lucy and Allison continued to discuss the day's adventure in whispers, Max promptly fell asleep.

The next morning, everyone had risen early – without too much grumbling – and made their breakfast. They'd been tired, so breakfast had vanished quickly, but all the girls were looking forward to making their way to the summit and the leaders hadn't had to do much prodding to get them to pack up and get ready for day two on the trail. After that, and with Max safely tucked away in Lucy's pack, the first few miles were over gentle terrain and the next two hours of backpacking passed pleasantly.

The rock slide, when it came, was terrifying.

It had started innocently enough, very high up - above The Scales, and near the summit of the mountain. In the stillness of the morning, a marmot had scurried along, looking for food. It had a regular routine for this, and knew this part of the mountain very well. On this particular day, however, as it scrambled over a rock that was not much larger than itself, the rock tipped to one side and began to slide. The rock only tipped by about thirty degrees, and it only slid about an inch and a half, but it was enough for it to collide with another rock.

In the short few moments that this took, the marmot had already moved along but, had it remained to watch – and had it been able to observe in slow motion – it would have been able to see a kind of rock ballet.

The second rock, which had also been rather precariously balanced, tipped to one side and slid just enough to encounter a third rock. The third rock tipped in a slightly different direction, slid and collided with two rocks. Of these, one rock as well situated and absorbed the blow without moving. The second one, however, slid into an inukshuk[9]. That's where the trouble really began.

The inukshuk, probably having been made by a passing backpacker that had stopped for a rest, had not been particularly well constructed so that, although it looked nice, when the third rock slid into it the whole structure collapsed, setting its other rocks into motion – all twenty of them. All of the rocks began to roll downhill, gathering momentum.

Even these rocks were quite unassuming. Only three or four of them were much larger than the passing marmot, and none of them rolled or slid more than half a foot downhill. Of the twenty rocks, only six or seven of them actually collided with others. It was, however, just enough to create a cascade.

Soon, more rocks were dislodging more rocks, and as the cascade continued, larger and larger rocks came into play. Their momentum increased, and the moving rocks took on the appearance of an opening fan.

The trickle of rocks had become a wave of rocks.

It would have ended there had not just enough rocks been moving just fast enough to cause a layer of shale to break free and begin to slide in a sheet that quickly broke up into dozens of rocks.

The wave of rocks had become a torrent!

What had begun as a modest sheet of rock and scree breaking away had become a torrent that gained speed and broadened its path as it continued downward. As it did so, clouds of dust were created and billowed up, and the sound of it all changed and increased in volume. Compared with the first few, slight clicking sounds of one rock sliding into another, the collective sounds of many rocks, tipping over, sliding, and crashing into each other took on the sound of a rushing waterfall.

The original marmot and all the other animals in the immediate area sensed it now, and instinctively fled.

Although some of the dislodged rocks careened off in more or less random directions, the majority of them followed a combination of the pull of gravity and the path of least resistance.

The path of least resistance was the Chilkoot Trail. For the same reason that the backpackers followed the trail upwards, most of the rocks now followed it downwards.

They were heading for The Scales.

The girls had been enjoying a rest break where they broke-out above the tree-line at Mile 14.5 (1.5 miles beyond Sheep Camp). After their break, Lucy had surreptitiously slipped Max back in to her pack, all of the girls had shouldered their packs, and they had just been about to resume their hike when they had heard a noise that sounded like the rumble of distant thunder. Then the sound had increased to a roar, and they'd realized it was something bad: an avalanche of snow, or rock, or both.

Almost immediately, the noise was accompanied by dust clouds so they could see where it was and where it might be headed.

That got them running!

The patrol immediately abandoned their backpacks and started running. Since the rockslide noises were coming from ahead of them and to their left, they ran to their right (heading approximately south) and they navigated their way over and around the rocky terrain until they reached the edge of the forest. They continued into the forest in the reasonable hope that the trees might protect them from the rocks. Some ran almost blindly through the brush, which slowed them down considerably and frequently leading to falls, while others – whether through luck or a greater degree of control and observation – followed game trails, which allowed them to run faster and generally without tripping. As a result, the patrol became more and more separated from each other the longer they ran.

Being unfamiliar with the area in general, and with avalanches and rockslides in particular, none of the group knew how far to go, they just knew they had to run. As a result, they ran as far as they could.

By the time the rock slide reached Sheep Camp it had

finally expended the last of its kinetic energy and come to a halt, some of the rocks and debris having passed through right where the girls had been resting! They didn't know this at the time though, as the patrol had kept on scrambling through the forest until they couldn't run any longer. When they did stop, the eerie silence signaled that the rock slide was over.

Unwilling to trust the sudden silence, the two leaders quickly decided to stay where they were for a while, in a small clearing, and to use the time to collect their patrol together. Since they had purposely not overtaken any of the running girls, they hoped that they would be able to simply remain in place and wait for the girls to backtrack to them. For the most part, this worked out quite well. After much calling out, the first two arrived almost immediately, followed by the stragglers, one, then another, then another.

Five of the girls, once they'd calmed down enough to provide coherent self-assessments seemed to be OK – they were bruised, tired, shaken, and scared, but bravely declared themselves to be "OK." That, however, was only five of the original patrol of six Guides.

"Has anyone seen Lucy?" Brown Owl[10] asked.

Silence.

It turned out that no one had seen Lucy since they'd all dropped their packs and started running.

They'd tried calling out for Lucy, but received no response. The leaders next tried sending the girls out in various directions, each heading along a different path or trail but always remaining in sight of another Guide or one of the leaders. This was a very smart thing to do, and a testament to the quality of the Guide leaders that they had come up with this plan without any prior training[11]. Unfortunately, this tactic didn't produce any results either.

Their next decision was to range forward, in case Lucy had outrun them all. In this case the two leaders had the girls stay together in the clearing, and went forward together, again calling out Lucy's name. This was also unsuccessful.

Running out of options, their next decision was to backtrack. With the girls spread out in a rough line, but such that each could see a patrol-member on each side of her, they worked their way back to the Chilkoot Trail. When they arrived, they found all of their backpacks were still where they had left them, dust-covered but intact, but there was still no sign of Lucy.

Where is she? they wondered.

Laurie Schramm

4 SILVER'S REUNION

Goldie, was about the same size as Silver, but had golden eyes, and reddish-golden colouring. It was easy to see how she had earned her name.

As we watched the vigorous reunion, Ross continued his explanation. "Goldie was born a few minutes before Silver here, but that was enough to establish her as the head of the litter. There were six puppies originally. We sold off the rest of them but had intended to keep Goldie and Silver for ourselves."

By this time, Silver and Goldie had stopped tussling and were simply standing, virtually nose-to-nose, gazing intently into each other's eyes. It was uncanny seeing them silently stare at each other like that. It reminded me of all the times that I'd looked into Silver's eyes and felt like I could tell what he was thinking, and for a moment... I had the sense that they were communicating in some way. This feeling was reinforced when they broke off and I felt – not just saw but felt – Goldie's penetrating gaze on me.

"Ross..." I began, still watching her intently.

"Yeah," Ross said, somewhat sheepishly. "We don't talk about that..."

Goldie padded forward to greet me, and I went down on my knees to meet her. I offered my hand for her to sniff, which she did, and then she surprised me by reaching up and licking my face.

As she was doing this I glanced over at Silver, who was looking at me very intently and I couldn't escape the feeling that I was being welcomed into a larger pack. My mind was filling with questions now but, before I could ask, a woman somewhat younger than Ross had come out of one of the buildings and walked up meet us.

"Hi! I'm Sally," was all she had time to say before Silver was there standing upright on his two back legs and licking her face.

It took a while for both dogs to decide that they'd completed enough licking for now, but eventually I was able to stand up, shake hands with Sally, and reiterate that I'd wanted to come and see where Silver had grown up.

It was decided that we should head back to the house and exchange some stories. As we walked back, Ross and Sally pointed out some other features of their place including a dog training run that looked a lot like a racetrack for horses, buggies, or even race cars, except that it was smaller. As we went by, I noticed that they even had summer sleds – dog sleds with wheels instead of skis, and which were clearly designed for dog team training in the summer months.

Reaching the house and being shown into their living room, I quickly discovered that the reunions weren't over yet. Two older dogs immediately rose from their blankets on the floor and together met with Silver. Whereas Silver and Goldie's reunion had mostly resembled a friendly wrestling match, Silver's meeting with what turned out to be his parents was more like a meeting of diplomats. As the three of them stood together, gazing intently at each other, nose to nose to nose I was reminded of childhood storybooks in which a King and Queen's knightly son would return home after a long absence in which he had grown to manhood.

I don't know exactly what put this thought into my head but it was quite prophetic, as Ross told me that these were Silver's parents: King and Queenie.

I immediately put my hand to my mouth in an attempt to hide my instinctive smile, but this turned out to be a futile gesture as I couldn't help breaking out into laughter as well: "King and Queenie, and Goldie and Silver?"

"Sure, what's wrong with that?" asked Sally, looking a bit mystified, and possibly wondering whether to be offended or not.

"It's just all too much," I said, still chuckling, "the coincidences I mean."

Now both Ross and Sally looked mystified. "Maybe I should tell you a bit of our story," I offered. With Silver still visiting with his parents, we all sat down and I told them a bit about my background and how I'd come to join the Mounted Police, then my first posting and how Silver and I had come to meet[5].

"Later on, Silver and I trained in the RCMP's dog service, so he's now a police dog and we're a team – both on the job and off," I concluded. "The reason I was laughing, was that part of the Mounties' Hollywood legacy is a whole series of shows and books about a fictional character known as Sergeant Preston of the Mounties and his faithful side-kick and ally, Yukon King, who was an Alaskan Malamute. Not only that – I don't know if you've ever seen any of the TV or book pictures of Yukon King, but he was the spitting image of your own dog King!"

Putting my two hands out, both King and Queenie padded over and each commandeered a hand for a prolonged sniffing session, after which they curled up at my feet looking quite contented.

Ross and Sally had heard of the Sergeant Preston character but weren't familiar with the stories, or his famous dog. They did, however, appreciate the multiple coincidences. Although they were naturally curious about Silver's and my adventures together, they also wanted to know about Norm.

"Norman Poole came to see us in 1974," Ross explained. "He told us that he was a hunting and fishing guide in Northern Saskatchewan, and that he was building a dogsled team and wanted a young dog that could lead the team."

"We hadn't been planning to sell Silver at all, but Norm seemed so dedicated to the spirit of dog-sledding, and like he'd be a good and considerate owner, that our resolve weakened. We couldn't keep all of our dogs, of course, so in the end we'd reluctantly agreed to sell Silver to him. Silver was only four years old then, but he'd already shown great promise, had been trained to pull a sled, and enjoyed it so much that he'd become a lead dog. Even most of the older dogs had already accepted his leadership in the harness traces. I think he enjoyed the relative independence of being in the front, and he was certainly the best I've ever seen at understanding the commands of the musher."

That had been the last time Ross and Sally had seen Norm or Silver.

"I think Norm would have been a good owner," I offered, explaining that I'd heard good things about the two of them, and that I'd gotten to know Norm fairly well during my posting to Radium City, where he'd lived. I also briefly related the sad tale of Norm's death, and how Silver's ownership had passed to Norm's friend, Ruby Gillespie, and then to me.

"Of course, by that time Silver had already attached himself to me and we'd become friends and partners," I finished.

Although they were saddened to hear of Norm's fate, they were pleased with the tale of Silver's and my history together, and especially pleased to be able to see Silver again. It was on this note that they made me an offer I couldn't refuse.

"Where are you staying?" Sally had asked.

"I don't really know," I responded. "I was actually going to ask you for a recommendation."

"Look, we have several tourist cabins here. We're normally full, but we just had a cancellation so we have an empty cabin available for tonight and tomorrow night. You're welcome to stay here for free if you want – meals included."

"Thank you, that sounds great! But I'm happy to pay for it."

"Tell you what," put in Ross. "Tell us some more stories while you're here, maybe pick up a bottle of wine or two for tomorrow, and we'll call it even – OK?"

I'd readily agreed, and Silver and I had spent two really enjoyable, and relaxing days with them during which a couple of really significant things happened. The first came up over dinner when Ross had been talking about why they loved Alaska and all the outdoor activities that were available. This provided my cue to ask about one of the things I'd always wondered about Silver.

"Do you know why he doesn't like to go into the water?"

This produced chuckling and a simultaneous "Yes" from both Ross and Sally.

"We laugh about it now," Ross explained, "but it was a serious thing at the time.

"It was a gorgeous Spring day and I was out with a team practising for a dog-sled race. Silver and Goldie were matched-up together, behind our most senior lead dog. Behind them were some of our younger, and less experienced, dogs. Things had been going well, and we had turned around and were on our way back home. About a mile from here we crossed the river, like we always do.

"With hindsight, there were more pressure ridges and cracks than normal for the time of year, but they were hidden under a light covering of snow. We learned later that there was also some kind of rise in the water level up-stream that caused another pressure surge. In any case, we were almost across the river. In fact, the lead dog, and Silver and Goldie, were already fully across when all of a sudden there was a tremendous 'crack' and the ice broke-up in large pieces, right underneath the sled. The sled twisted upwards and began to sink, putting even more pressure on an uplifted sheet of ice, which promptly broke apart, and before I could react, the sled dropped right down into the water, dragging the whole dog team with it.

"It took me a long time to get at all the dogs and cut them free and, in every case, a terrified dog had been completely immersed for at least a moment before I was able to get them out. Silver and Goldie had the worst of it. They never forgot and neither of them would ever go in the water again!"

"Wow," I remarked. "That must have been terrifying for all of you. I always found it odd that Silver really doesn't mind getting wet but never wants to go in the water – now I can understand why."

At this point Silver gave a grave sort of "yip," as if in agreement.

"But now I need to tell you a new story that involved Silver being thrown into the water again," I continued.

Although I left out some of the most interesting details, which were either national security, or highly personal secrets, I related the essence of the story[12] of how Silver, and a colleague, and I had been out on a converted fishing boat off Cape Breton Island, Nova Scotia. The boat had struck something in the water and immediately begun to sink. This had the effect of dumping us all into the frigid Atlantic Ocean and requiring us to swim to a nearby island, find some rudimentary shelter, and survive a highly uncomfortable night before being rescued by a fisherman the following morning.

Even without the juicy details, Ross and Sally were suitably impressed and sympathetic. Once again, Silver and Goldie had been watching closely during the telling of this story, which provided the segue to the second really significant thing.

"By the way," I began, "is it just me, or have you ever had the impression that Silver understands more about human speech than can really be possible?"

There was a long silence. I waited, as Ross turned to look at Sally, who gave him a significant but indecipherable (to me) look. With a sigh, Ross shifted in his chair, seemed to struggle with how to begin, and then clearly decided to just let it out.

"You asked me something like this when we were watching Silver's reunion with Goldie," he began.

"Yes, and then you said something to the effect that you don't talk about it."

"Well, yes, that's right. We don't talk about it because we don't want people to think we're crazy." Then, thinking about what he'd just said, he amended, "or, at least any crazier than they already think we are." This produced smiles all around, and I let another silence play out – waiting for him to continue.

"Well," Ross sighed, "it all started when Queenie had the litter of pups that produced Goldie, Silver, and their siblings. Everything seemed normal at first, but over time it often seemed like Goldie and Silver could communicate with each other somehow. In addition to all the usual playing, sometimes we'd notice them staring intently at each other, after which they'd go off and do something together. There was no way to be sure, but we eventually got the distinct impression that they were communicating – or at least had a remarkable understanding of each other."

"You'd never seen this before?" I asked.

"Not like this, and we've raised over 60 sled-dogs here. There are always dogs that bond with some more closely than with others, and some that learn faster than others, but something always seemed different with these two... and then there was the time they tried it on me!"

"On you?"

"Yes. I'd been out on a practice run with a sled and a team that included Goldie and Silver. Once again, I had matched the two of them up, right behind the lead dog. On the way back home, I'd decided to try following a game trail through the forest, which I really should not have done since it was late in the day."

Ross paused and sighed. "Anyway, I lost my way in the forest and eventually came to a fork in the trail. It was late in the day, and the sky was cloudy, so the light was poor, and I hadn't brought a compass with me. I wasn't sure which way to turn, but my instinct was to follow the fork to the right. As I tried to get the team moving in that direction, both Goldie and Silver dug their paws in, and refused to mush. As I yelled at them to get going, they simply stood there straining at their harnesses.

"At this point, I was mystified more than angry. Nothing like this had ever happened before with these two dogs. When I finally hesitated, unsure what to do next, both of them turned to stare at me with incredibly penetrating gazes that seemed to say 'Not this way!' I wondered whether I was just imagining things, but some inner instinct persuaded me to pay attention and follow their lead.

"They were right, of course. The trail my instincts wanted me to follow led completely the wrong way and, I later discovered, would have led to an impassable ridge of rock that would have left us far from home, with darkness falling. To this day, I have no idea how they knew which trail to take, nor how they were able to communicate that to me... Anyway, that was the first time, but there have been others. It's always subtle, so subtle that you can easily convince yourself that it's only your imagination, but I've come to believe that there are times when they can sense my thoughts, and times when they can communicate simple thoughts to me – only Goldie and Silver, never any of the other dogs. I think they somehow inherited some abilities that may have been more common in their ancestors.

"The aboriginal tribes have some interesting traditional stories about wolves. In some of those stories, wolves are fierce, unpredictable rulers of the forests that humans need to beware. But in other stories wolves were pinnacles of courage, strength, hunting skill, and loyalty. One of my favourite stories is about how one wolf, back at the dawn of human evolution, was the original brother and best friend of the first man. That wolf, is said to have had powerful instincts, keen intuition, high intelligence, and a rudimentary ability to communicate with humans as well as other wolves.

"I like that one because you can tell just by looking at them that Alaskan Malamutes, like Silver here, aren't far removed from their Arctic Wolf ancestors, and they have a heritage as sled dogs that goes back at least two thousand years. What's more, the best of our dogs have been true best friends of ours."

"You said communicate. Communicate how?"

"I don't really know. The traditional knowledge stories only say that the original man and the original wolf had ways of understanding each other. I asked an elder, from one of our local aboriginal communities, about that once and she said it was probably a version of what people now call telepathy. Now do you get why we don't talk about this? No one believes in the occult anymore!"

"No," I said slowly, "but everything you've said matches my experiences with Silver. When he first saved my life, his sudden appearance scared the hell out of me, but as I gazed into his eyes, he seemed to want me to reach out and grab on to him. Fortunately, I was desperate enough to try it, and he saved me. Ever since then there have been many times when he has seemed to know what I'm thinking or saying, or that I seem to know what he's thinking."

"There you are then," said Ross, sounding relieved. "You're just as crazy as we are."

"What do you think?" I asked, turning to face Silver, who seemed to have been intently observing our conversation, "Are we all crazy?"

At this, Silver promptly rose up, padded over to me and placed his head in my lap. As I stroked behind his ears and looked into his eyes, I could feel a wave of emotion I can only describe as kinship. Looking back at Ross and Sally, I said, "I'm just so grateful that we found each other. Thank you for sharing your stories with me."

A very distinct stomach rumbling from Ross broke the spell, and Ross tried to defend himself against Sally's and my laughter by explaining that he was hungry and we should eat. At this, he and Sally promptly got up to start preparing dinner. They refused to hear of me pitching in to help, but with four dogs to visit with I was well occupied.

We finished the evening sitting outdoors, in companionable intervals of light conversation interspersed by periods of silence that allowed me to soak in the rugged

Alaskan mountain beauty.

5 AN INHUMAN MOUNTIE

Here is Silver's story[13]:

My Beginnings*. It was cold where I grew up. Even the summers had chilly nights, especially when the wind was up. The winters, however, were what defined the true meaning of cold…*

When it was well beyond the point when water would freeze solid, you learned early not to put your tongue on bare metal. Not more than once, anyway. The pain of feeling a layer of skin tear off of your tongue is the kind of pain that you never, ever, forget.

Our immediate family: my father, mother, sister and I, were all close. Unnaturally close, some said. At first, I had no idea what that meant. Later, I took it to be a jealous response to how happy our little family was together. It was much later, as I began to grow in maturity as well as size, that it dawned on me that my family communicated with each other somewhat differently than we did with others. It was a subtle thing with my parents, but something much stronger with my sister.

From my very first memories as a youngster, I remember being able to gaze into my sister Goldie's eyes and get – not her actual thoughts – but an image in my mind of what she was thinking. The same thing seemed to work for her too, but in reverse. For

43

example, I might gaze into her eyes and get a clear image of a field with a ball lying in the centre of it. **She wants to go play with the ball**, *I would think. Then, if I thought about the field and the ball, she would know that I was agreeing and we'd both simply get up and go play.*

I soon realized that when playing with others of my age, I couldn't understand them in the same way that I could my sister or parents. It's not that I couldn't communicate with others. It was more that our communications weren't as detailed, or as rich. Like the difference between looking out over a forested valley in the bluish illumination of twilight compared with looking at the same scene with the illumination of the late morning sun on a clear day. Like the difference between seeing a single colour compared with a rainbow. I didn't think much of it for the longest time.

***

Home, when I was growing up, was a large, fenced-in area with a large house, a barn, and quite a few smaller houses. My parents were servants, basically, and we lived in one of the small houses. We had a master and a mistress, who lived in the big house. They were kind to us, and I think we all liked them.

One of the other humans was a very old man. I never quite figured out what his duties were supposed to be, but there was no question about his place in our social structure. He was the Elder. He wasn't in charge of anything, such was the province of the master and mistress, but everyone treated him with respect. Even the master and the mistress. Even my playmates, and my sister, and I instinctively deferred to him. At the time I didn't clearly understand why that should be so. He had no authority over us, and even if he had, we were an immature and disrespectful bunch of children. But not to the Elder.

Although my playmates treated the Elder with respect, their relationship went no further. The Elder spoke to us all, but my playmates were never interested in what he had to say. They did not understand him.

For some reason, it was different for my sister and I. We would listen to him and, at first, we did not understand him either, but as time went on, we understood more and more and became ever more captivated. Just like between Goldie and I, we both found that we could understand more of the Elder's stories if we gazed directly into his eyes as he told them. As we came to understand what he was saying to us, we learned that he was descended from the very first peoples to have inhabited the area where I grew up. It hadn't occurred to me that there might have been a time before people.

There was something beyond our growing ability to understand him, however. Looking back, I think now that my sister and I sensed in him something special, something desirable, something that seemed elusive and unreachable. It was more than knowledge, although he certainly had that in abundance. I think we sensed wisdom.

It was his stories that called out to my sister and I. We would gather around him at every opportunity when he was in the mood to tell us stories – which, to be fair, was most of the time. We would sit at his feet and listen as he told us stories. These were stories from the past, some from the very distant past, and they were filled with interesting characters and adventures. As time went on, I began to perceive that each of the Elder's stories also contained knowledge, and very often a moral or some kind of wisdom. As the last two were of no interest to us at that age, it was a testament to the Elder's storytelling ability that we were drawn into the stories despite our growing awareness that he wasn't entertaining us, he was teaching us. By the time I knew this to be true, it was nowhere near enough to keep me away. I loved to hear his stories, and to watch them unfold in my mind's eye as each story was told.

The 'knowledge stories' told us about the environment in which we lived, and often focused on the different kinds of animals that surrounded us: birds, fish, deer, bears, and so on. Our instincts already told us which we could ignore, which we could hunt, and which to fear. He taught us to look deeper than that. The Elder's favourite stories involved the raven, which he identified as the creator of all things, the one that taught humans and animals alike to hunt. Above all, the raven was the most adventurous of beings. Most of the Elder's stories took us into the relationships among the animals. In one story for example, the Elder described how wolves would hunt and kill the weaker members of a herd of deer. Without the weak to slow them down, the herd was then faster — and more nimble - enabling the bulk of the herd to better avoid predators of all kinds and therefore survive and reproduce. In this way both species could not only co-exist but benefit from each other. I liked stories like that.

My favourite stories, in fact, involved the wolves.

The wolves of the Elder's stories were mythological, of course. Even at a young age I understood that. Nevertheless, my imagination soared with the ebb and flow of the stories as the best of the wolves exhibited, not just great hunting abilities, but courage, strength, and loyalty. The Elder's stories also taught that wolves and humans are closely related to each other, and that humans and dogs actually descended from wolves long, long ago. In several of the very best stories, a wolf and a human were siblings and/ or each other's best friend, and their adventures were strongly overlain by concepts like honour, wisdom, and destiny. These latter were new ideas for me, they sent my imagination racing.

When these stories were told I always wanted to be the wolf, of course, and as more and more of these stories were told they developed in me a yearning to have a destiny like the best of wolves. Like the best of wolves, I would be courageous, strong, loyal, wise, and honourable. The Elder surely intended something like this to happen, although I doubt that he'd have expected the depths to which such concepts would take root in my developing mind. Regardless, he was surely effective.

To this day, after all these years, I still strive to be like the best of the wolves in the Elder's stories. Even so, it's aspirational rather than real. That's because I'm not actually a wolf.

I'm told that I look like a wolf though, so perhaps I'm not so far removed after all.

You wouldn't be able to pronounce the name my parents gave me.

Our master named me Silver.

My sister Goldie and I spent so much time listening to the Elder's stories that, as time progressed, we eventually gained a better understanding of what our master and mistress (whose human names were Ross and Sally) were trying to communicate when they spoke to us. I don't mean their language, exactly, although we did learn quite a few of their words. It was more that we somehow understood more and more of the meaning of what they were trying to say to us.

*If, for example, one of them were to say: "Silver, go get your toy," I could understand that as "**Silver ??? get ??? toy**," because I understood those three words out of the five. This was not remarkable, as any of our other playmates would also have had the same understanding of this command.*

If, on the other hand, one of them were to say to the other: "The barometer is falling and I think we're in for a storm. I'm worried about it because we might get caught in a fierce downpour. I think we should take our raincoats with us and keep an eye on the weather while we're out in the fields," I might only recognize the words "storm" and "fields," but I would also have felt the apprehension conveyed and somehow understand the warning to be watchful of the weather. Our playmates would have caught the same two words and some sense of the emotion involved, but they would not have gained the other nuances. Goldie and I didn't know what to make of this, but it must have made our lives richer, more colourful in a sense, and it seems to have accelerated our learning of more and more of our human's words.

I think I was just about fully grown when Goldie and I learned that we could convey much more than growls, whines, and barks back to our humans. This came about quite unexpectedly but at a very important time.

Our master and mistress had begun to train us to join with other dogs in pulling a heavy thing made mostly of wood from trees. They called it a sled, and it was supported on long strips of wood called skis. Each of us would wear a harness connected to a central lead that was, in turn, connected to the sled. Then, working together, we could pull the sled over the snow even if it had things loaded on it and a human standing on the back of it. Pulling our share of the load was work, but it was also exhilarating to be part of a team, to be able to run, and to be able to get out and away from our familiar surroundings and out into wilder country.

Anyway, one day we were out with the master, pulling the sled. Goldie and I were positioned side-by side, as we had been promoted to the two positions immediately following the lead dog. This was a big step for us, but the lead dog was very experienced, demanding but even tempered, and all we had to do was watch him carefully and follow his lead. I thought that our run had gone very well, and we had clearly reached its limit and had turned around, back towards home. When we were part of the way back, our master decided to try following a game trail through the forest.

It was late in the day, and the sky was cloudy, so the light was poor. Maybe that contributed to the problem, but for whatever reason, when we came to a fork in the trail our master signalled for us to turn towards the right and take that path. Our lead dog seemed fine with this and began to pull in that direction, but Goldie suddenly flashed an image into my mind: this was not the path that led towards home. We both remembered being there before, and knew that the path to the right led off in almost exactly the wrong direction and would have led to an impassable ridge of rock that would have left us far from home, with darkness falling.

Since my sense of direction, and of what lie ahead on each fork in the trail, matched Goldie's I sent a confirming image back to her.

Now what?

It was winter. It was cold. We both knew that we couldn't afford to take the wrong trail. Not knowing what else to do, we both dug our paws into the snow and refused to mush.

That wasn't fun. Our master started yelling at us, and the lead dog started barking and snapping at us, but we both had the strongest feeling that it was the left-hand path that would take us home. Caught between our senses and our duty to obey, we both stood there frozen, straining at our harnesses. This seemed to catch our master by surprise. He stopped yelling and stared at us, looking more puzzled than angry. It was as if he was trying to understand what was bothering us.

*Not knowing what else to do, Goldie and I simply stood there and stared directly at our master, trying to see into his eyes and to communicate the sense of danger we sensed. We tried to use our minds to project a sense of what we would say to him, if we could, which would have been: "***Not this way!***"*

Unbelievable as it may seem, he seemed to get the essence of what we were trying to communicate.

What an amazing thing, *I thought.*

To make a long story short, our master decided to try the fork that Goldie and I wanted to take, gave the appropriate instructions to our lead dog, and we made it home, safe and sound. Our master was good enough to recognize that we'd been right, and was very appreciative. Goldie and I were able to lounge in front of the big fireplace in the great house, and soak up the restoring warmth, water, food, and treats.

The master must have told the Elder about our adventure, because the next time we sat at his feet to listen, he told stories about the ancestry of dogs like Alaskan Malamutes, which was the humans' name for our family. The Elder taught us that we had a long heritage that spanned a multitude of generations, that we were descended from the Arctic Wolves, and that our ancestors were the original siblings and best friends of the very first humans. Those original wolves, the Elder taught, had the ability to communicate — or at least to be able to exchange understandings - with humans, as well as with other wolves.

I don't know about Goldie, but these stories inspired in me a desire to push the boundaries and see how far this communication thing with humans could be developed.

There was another sled-pulling trip with our master that was to have a life-long effect on me, and on my attitude towards water.

Once again, we were out with the master and working together to pull the sled. As before, Goldie and I were positioned side-by side, and immediately following the lead dog. We'd had another good run and we had clearly reached its limit and had turned around, back towards home. When we were most of the way back there was a frozen river we had to cross. This we had done many times before, and I thought nothing of it beyond the fact that the pads on my paws didn't grip as well on ice as they did in snow. This caused a certain amount of slipping around, but I'd learned to keep my balance well enough to avoid running into any of my companions. What happened next was a complete surprise, however.

We were crossing a river when all of a sudden there was a tremendous 'crack' and the ice broke-up in large pieces, right underneath the sled. Almost immediately, the sled dropped right down into the water, dragging the whole dog team with it.

We'd almost made it across the river, and the lead dog, and Goldie and I had even managed to reach the shore when we felt a massive pull from behind us. As I yelped and turned my head, I could see that the ice had broken open, the sled was twisted upwards in to the air, and some of it was already well underwater. Despite our best efforts to move forward, the pull on our harnesses was too great to overcome and we were all pulled back from the shore, back across the ice, and back toward the hole. It was terrifying.

Our master had jumped off the sled and started cutting the other dogs free, but it took a long time. By the time he got to Goldie and I, we'd been repeatedly pulled under the water and each time had to struggle up to get our heads beck up above water so we could breathe. He worked on Goldie's harness before mine, and he was helping to keep her nose and mouth above water at the same time. I approved but, if anything, that made it worse for me, as I was repeatedly being either dragged or pushed under water for longer and longer periods of time.

I don't know how anyone can describe the feeling of drowning without actually experiencing it. My feelings were a combination of horror and panic. I had an overwhelming urge to open my mouth and take in air, but I knew that to open my mouth would only bring in water. My chest and throat would spasm in a desperate, instinctive attempt to get air. At the same time, I would have to clamp my mouth shut in a similarly desperate attempt to prevent me from inhaling water. These roughly equal but opposite forces had me heaving back and forth at the same time as a sense of panic rose up in me. It... was... horrible.

I kept struggling, of course, and I'm sure my eyes were wild with fright, but I knew that our master was doing his best to save us, so I tried to avoid panicking long enough for him to get Goldie and I free. Eventually, and just about when I'd been so starved for air that I was on the verge of blacking out, he got my harness cut and gave me a huge push up onto the ice.

All I could do, for a while, was lie there taking in huge gulps of air.

A few minutes after that, and it was all over.

By the time our master had released the lead dog and dragged himself up onto the shore, our team had mostly calmed down and shaken ourselves out. After that, we all just walked home -

shivering all the way. When we got there, our master and mistress were sufficiently worried about us that they let us all into the great room of the main house, wet fur and all, so we could curl up in front of their roaring fireplace.

What a contrast that was to the icy water in which we'd all nearly drowned!

Most of my companions shrugged the experience off. Maybe none of them had spent as much time fully immersed as I had. I don't know. What I do know is that the experience left me with a perpetual fear of drowning. I never forgot, I never shed the horror, and as I re-live these memories again, I find myself shuddering.

I never willingly went into the water again.

Now, I need to explain my relationships with two other humans that changed my world forever. While growing up, I noticed that as others of our pack had become full grown and had learned to work as part of a team pulling sleds, then strangers would come and look them over. Sooner or later, one of the strangers would make some kind of arrangement with the master and mistress such that the stranger was to become their new master and they would go off with them, never to be seen again.

There was a day when this happened to me.

I'd been lounging on the roof of our family's small house when another stranger showed up to look over all of us that were young but full grown, of which we numbered five at that particular time. Our master didn't introduce him to me at first, only the other four, but the stranger didn't seem impressed with any of them for some reason and kept looking over at me and pointing. Initially, my master just shook his head, as if to say "no" but as they continued their discussion he eventually relented and brought him over to introduce us.

"Silver, this is Norm. Come down and say hello," my master said, by way of introduction.

I jumped down from my rooftop perch and padded over. The male named Norm held out his hand for inspection and I gave him a careful sniff and then looked deeply into his eyes. I didn't sense anything concerning in his scent, or his manner, or his mind, but I didn't find anything very interesting there either. As we stood there, Norm and my master continued what was obviously a prior conversation that had them both talking in animated fashion. I could tell that they were discussing sleds, sled-pulling, and sled racing, and I immediately sensed that they were kindred spirits — in sled racing at least.

I couldn't understand everything they were saying, of course, but when Norm spoke, I got an image of a sled racing through beautiful snow-covered country, a team of dogs, and- to my amazement — he clearly imagined me at the head of the team as lead dog.

That sounded interesting. I'd never been put in the lead position before, although I'd watched enough other lead dogs to have some understanding of the job.

Eventually the master, with some reluctance, seemed to reach an agreement with Norm. They shook hands, and then the master knelt-down by my head and said: "Silver, you're going to be going away with Norm here. He'll be your new master now."

And that was that.

I travelled to a new home with Norm in his 'truck' machine. The journey took many, many cycles of the sun and moon — more cycles than I have claws on my two front paws. Norm's home was not only far away but in a place of quite different geography. There were no mountains, for one thing, just hills. The waters were different, too. Instead of one huge body of undrinkable water — what my former masters had referred to as ocean — there were many smaller bodies of drinkable water, called lakes. Some of them were quite large, but nothing on the scale of the ocean. Also, the forests were quite sparse compared with what I was used to.

Norm's place was similar to that of my previous master and mistress except that everything was smaller. There were quite a few dogs already there, and I was given my own little house with a roof I could lounge on. I kind of liked having my own house, but it was lonely being away from my sister and parents. Not far away from Norm's place was a whole community of human houses. Norm and the other humans referred to it as Radium City.

As a master, Norm was fine. His voice and manner often sounded rough, but he treated his dogs well. The other dogs were fine too. There was no real pack leader when I arrived, but I think there must have been one before. The other dogs accepted me and I them. We had time to play, time to lounge, and then there was the sledding.

If there was one thing we had in common, it was the enjoyment of sledding. Norm dropped me into the leader's traces right from the start. None of the other dogs did more than grumble a bit, and I was somewhat surprised to find that leading worked out just fine. I had to be vigilant, and keep my team-mates in line, but this didn't usually require more than sharp barks, the odd growl, and the occasional nip. I had no trouble at all in understanding Norm's commands as the musher. I didn't understand all of his words, of course, but I always seemed to be able to read the image in his mind, so the two of us were almost always in perfect alignment. Our sled runs, as a result, were amazing fun.

It was through Norm that I was introduced to a way to explore the larger bodies of water without getting wet. Norm called it a boat. In the warmer months, when the water was ice-free, Norm would take people out — one or two at a time — across the big lake to places where they could hunt for larger animals or fish. For some reason, he fell into the habit of bringing me along on such trips. Although I was initially nervous of the possibility of falling into the water, or of the boat sinking, my fears turned out to be groundless, and I learned to enjoy the experience. As the boat made its way over the water, I found that I could observe the changing scenery, smell the complex smells brought by the wind, and relish the freedom of being able to do it all from the comfort of the boat. All without having to do any work!

One day, when Norm went out on the lake, it was just the two of us. After some time, we reached land and Norm pulled the boat up on shore. From there we went for a walk that brought us to a hill, a hill with a cave.

It was obvious that the cave had been made by humans. The floor was smooth and flat, the roof and walls looked un-natural, and it had the smell of machinery. Norm had brought a light with him, and we walked deep inside. Norm called it a mine.

It was cool and damp in the mine. From somewhere up ahead I could hear water dripping. Eventually, the floor changed to wood - something like my master had in his house. Just beyond that, the mine widened and came to an end. Norm took off his outer layer of clothing and hung it from a piece of rock that stuck out from one wall, then he sat down. He seemed to be thinking, so I sat down beside him and curled up to rest.

After a few minutes, my head instinctively popped up as I heard noises coming from the entrance to the mine. I smelled a familiar scent: it was the human named Jim. Jim lived in the same general area that we did, he also had a boat, and I had observed that he spent a lot of his time out on the lake taking other humans — mostly males — out on the big lake.

Jim, I did not like. Until now, I've described relationships with humans that varied from good, such as with Norm, to great, such as with my former master and mistress, to reverent, such as with the Elder. All of my senses and abilities that came together in my head to produce the welcome, colourful impressions of these people, turned against me with certain other humans. Jim is an example. From my very first meeting with him my senses were in conflict. My eyes provided information, but nothing negative or concerning. My ears heard a pleasant voice, and again, nothing in the parts of Jim's speech that I could understand caused me concern. If anything, his conversations with Norm seemed to be very amicable. All of my other senses, however, rebelled at the notion of any kind of contact with Jim. I sensed... a brooding anger, resentment even. Against what, I have never known. I sensed... a darkness in his mind that worried me.

When Jim came into view and greeted Norm, they talked for a while. As nearly as I could judge, they were talking about searching for something valuable. The images in both of their minds seemed to be of a kind of shiny metal that could be broken out of a special kind of rock.

Although prudence advised caution and an outward display of indifference, if not polite companionship, I did not — and to some extent still do not — have enough control over my instincts to prevent my ears from flattening back and a low growl from emerging. This, of course, was promptly noticed by both Norm and Jim, with the former instructing me to back-off and the latter taking a step back and keeping his distance from me. For my part, I did my best to stay close to Norm and be alert for trouble.

When Norm and Jim's conversation concluded, they began walking out of the mine. When we emerged into the light, we walked down to the water. There, beside Norm's boat, was Jim's larger boat. Jim climbed into his boat and motioned for Norm to join him. Then, some kind of argument began, in which they raised their voices and waved their hands, with Jim pointing at me. The core of it seemed to be that Jim wanted Norm to get into the boat without me.

Norm then knelt down beside me and said something like: "Silver... boat... stay." He looked directly into my eyes as he spoke, and the image I received in my mind was that he was trying to tell me that he would come back for me. Then, reminding me to "stay," he got into Jim's boat and they headed out on the lake.

As ordered, I curled up by the shore and waited for Norm to return, but I never saw Norm alive again.

It was a long wait, and when the sun had moved across a significant portion of the sky, I trotted up the big hill with the mine in it, so I could get a better view. From my vantage point on top of the hill, I could also see that the land I was on was surrounded on all sides by water. I was trapped!

Where was Norm?, I wondered.

I know now that I could have tried swimming. I've seen other dogs and wolves swim in water, but at that age I didn't know whether I could swim or not. That, added to my horror of water, plus the fact that I couldn't actually see land anywhere - even from the top of the hill - made me think I should stay put.

For most of the rest of the day, I went back to the top of the hill and resumed my vigil, watching for Norm's return. Although there was no food, there was water, and I occasionally trotted down to the lake for a drink. By the time the sun was beginning to disappear into the distance it was becoming cool and windy, so I went back into the mine and curled up near Norm's clothing, hoping that he would return.

When the sun rose into the sky again, I went out and back down to the water. There was still no sign of Norm. Once again, I went to the top of the hill to watch and wait for Norm. When the sun was high in the sky, I went back to the mine and curled up for a nap near Norm's clothing.

I was woken from my nap by the sounds of someone coming into the mine. There were flashes of light from a hand-held light, and I caught the scent of an unfamiliar human female. She had an interesting scent. Not sensing any danger, and curious about this stranger, I stayed curled-up where I was and waited.

As the woman came slowly forward, I began to sense fragments of her thought. She was being careful, she was searching for something, and I began to detect indications of compassion and a fine mind. As I remained curled up, with my ears up and pointing forward, and my nose doing the same, my sense gathering was interrupted by a loud "crack - snap" sound of wood breaking. At *almost the same instant, the woman came into my sight and gave out a sharp "Eeek!" sound as the floor below her gave way and most of her dropped out of sight into a large hole that had opened-up in the floor.*

As I blinked in surprise, I saw that she had not completely fallen into the hole. Her head and arms were visible at the top edge of the hole. The rest of her body must have been hanging straight down in to the hole because she was trying to use small movements of her arms to prevent herself from falling completely.

I'm sure she didn't see me yet, that came later, but I could see straight into her eyes. That, combined with the intensity of her thoughts, gave me startlingly clear impressions of her thoughts.

She was afraid, trying to avoid panic, and trying to control her breathing. At the same time, she was trying to figure out how to escape the hole. This reminded me so much of my experience when I was dragged into the water when my former master's sled fell through the ice, that I felt strong surges of empathy and sympathy for her.

Continuing to watch — and sense - the drama before me, I was fascinated by her attempts to stay in control of her emotions and think her way out of trouble. My eyes, ears, nose, and mental perceptions all combined to give me a deep understanding of her efforts. Although my eyes could only see a small amount of her, I could sense through her mind's eye her efforts to find supports for her feet or other parts of her body, trying to find something she could grab with her hands, and trying to shift here self to one side or the other, but nothing worked. It wasn't long before I detected new emotions from her: she was getting tired.

She called "Help!" several times, so there was apparently another human outside the mine somewhere, but whoever it was, they never came. I could tell that she was continuing to tire.

There was something compelling about this person, I sensed intelligence, persistence, a spirit of adventure, and a spirit of purpose about her. I was suddenly reminded of the Elder's stories of the first human and the first wolf and I realized with a start that I could not just lie there and let her fall, possibly to her death.

At the same time as I sensed that she was bracing herself to try something desperate, I leapt to my paws. In two bounds, I was right in front of her, and I called out: "Grruph, grruph, grruph."

That got her attention! She was so startled that she nearly lost her balance on the edge of the hole. I could sense that I had unintentionally frightened her, but she recovered herself quickly.

I stared straight onto her eyes, and gave a couple of neutral barks, trying to get her attention. When I could see her examining me with a puzzled, but wary, look on her face I lowered my shoulders and put my head down on the rock floor, between my front legs and paws, in the universal sign — among dogs and wolves at least — of non-aggression.

Although this behaviour continued to mystify her, she did get the message that she needn't be afraid of me. She also looked straight into my eyes. That was the opportunity I wanted, and I tried to send her an image of grabbing the loose fur at the back of my neck, so I could try to help pull her out.

"You ??? ??? me," she said out loud. I don't know all the words she said, but I got the message of amazement and almost amused disbelief.

As we continued to share our gaze, I kept trying to send an image of her grabbing my fur so I could help her get up and over the edge of the hole. At the same time, I received clearer impressions from her mind that I have ever received from any human. It was amazing!

Although I knew that she was having trouble believing what was happening to her, she was tiring rapidly now and I could feel the exact moment when she decided that she had no other options, and nothing to lose by taking the risk of grabbing me. And that's exactly what she did. She slowly moved one arm over to me and lifted her hand up and on top of my neck. At this, I gave a sniff and kept staring at her, so she grabbed my fur and moved her other arm slightly in preparation for a push upward. At this, I gave a snort, meaning "**about time**," braced myself, and lifted my head and shoulders. She held on tight, so I next started to shift my body back a bit.

I could sense that she was fully with me now, and the two of us alternately shifted this way and that so she could use her free arm to rise up a bit. That allowed me to lower my head again and use my jaws to grab her clothing. Now that we each had a solid grip on the other, I did my best to back up while she worked at levering more and more of her body up and over the edge of the hole. It wasn't long before we got her upper body over the edge, and after that she was able to swing the lower part of her body up and over the edge.

I could feel waves of relief coming from her, as she let go of my fur, rolled onto her back, and lay there taking in large breaths. After a moment she rolled over onto her side, looked straight into my eyes and said, "Thank you. I ??? know ??? came from ??? thank you!" I only got some of the words, but it was very clear what she was thinking.

When she got her breath back, and her heart rate had slowed, it was interesting to watch what she did next. Rather than quickly leave, she carefully stepped around the big hole and examined our surroundings. She found, and seemed to be very interested, in Norm's clothing. She even smelled it and I could sense her identify the scent as belonging to someone she knew. It reminded her of a home she had been in. Her mental image of that home, and the home's smells, was so clear that I knew without doubt that she had identified the clothing's owner as Norm.

This was amazing. Not only was this the first human I'd ever encountered that used all of her senses, but she had identified the clothing's scent as belonging to Norm! A woman with wolf-like qualities!

Next, she recovered her light and used it to carefully examine the hole. Again, I was able to follow the gist of her thoughts. These *ranged from curious, as she investigated, to surprise and anger, as she realized that she had fallen into a trap. This produced so many questions in her mind that I could no longer isolate and identify any of them, but one thing came through clearly: she was determined to find out more. Accordingly, she started walking back out of the mine. Curious, and strangely attracted, I followed along.*

Exiting the mine, the woman walked around the hill until she came across a man sitting near the second mine. It was Jim!

Jim seemed surprised to see the woman, and as they talked to each other I sensed frustration and suspicion in her. At some point their conversation came around to me, and I heard my name mentioned.

"Him ??? Silver ??? Norm ??? sled dogs," I heard Jim say.

The woman and Jim continued to talk, and I eventually heard Jim say her human name: Alex. Then they went around everywhere, as if searching for something. I heard Norm's name mentioned so often that I decided they must be searching for him. I thought that was strange, since Norm had gone away with Jim to begin with. My suspicions of Jim deepened.

As they searched around, I more or less followed along, keeping an eye on them. When they reached Jim's boat, it was clear that they were planning to leave. I sensed that Alex wanted to bring me with them. I would have stayed and hoped for Norm's return, but I was reluctant to leave Alex, partly because she fascinated me, and partly because I felt the need to protect her from Jim. The final thing was my sense that she was actually intent on finding Norm. This gave us a common cause, so when she turned to me and said: "Come Silver, ??? boat!" I simply, walked down to the shore, gave Jim a glance, and jumped into the boat.

As Jim directed the boat out across the big lake, Alex offered me some of her food. Feeling starved, I didn't hesitate, and the food quickly vanished. I took the fact that she was willing to share her food with me as another good sign. The rapid infusion of food made me sleepy and, not sensing any immediate action or threat, I curled up on the seat behind Alex and dropped-off to sleep.

When it was time to leave the boat, Alex signaled for me to join her in a truck like Norm's, but which was clearly hers. I hopped in. She drove me home, but there was no one there. Not Norm, and not even any of the other dogs. I thought that was strange, and so did Alex: I could sense that she felt suspicious. I stayed with her as she drove to where other humans often collected, and to where Norm's boat was tied, and finally to where Alex lived. She let me explore her house, and as I sniffed around, I realized that I found her scent strike some kind of chord in me. Something about being with her felt right and, since we were both looking for Norm, I decided that I would continue to stay with her if I could.

When the sun went down, she went for a long walk around the area of the human's houses and I stayed close. I enjoyed being with her and I sensed that she felt appreciative of my company. After that, she tried to leave me outside for the night, but I made it clear that I was unhappy with that idea. I wanted to be inside with her. I had a feeling that I should be protecting her, so I definitely didn't want to be left outside. Fortunately, she relented and let me in, and I lost no time in establishing myself at the foot of her bed for the night.

When the sun next rose, Alex went around the area again, but running this time. That was more fun!

I found that I could run off on my own from time to time, to investigate interesting smells, then run back to catch-up with her, accompany her for a while, and then head off again to other interesting spots. I enjoyed being with her, and I sensed that she enjoyed my company as well. Later, I followed her to various places where she talked to other people, and I sensed that she was still on the hunt for Norm.

For more rising and settings of the sun I followed Alex as she talked to more and more humans in her search for information about Norm. At one point, she looked at me and said: '???

Silver, ??? go visit ??? more ???" In her mind I sensed a trip over waters and more caves or mines: she was planning to search further away for Norm.

"Grruph," I said.

"Yes, we ??? be careful ..." she said. I agreed.

We took one more boat trip out on the big lake to see a different cave, or mine, this time. This time, working together, we found Norm – but Norm was dead. I sat down with a low whine. Poor Norm, I thought.

"I??? sorry Silver," Alex said, as she did her own checks to verify that Norm was dead. Then she sat back on her heels and gave me a hug, saying *"I??? afraid Norm ??? gone."*

Then she did a strange thing. Alex turned Norm's body over and continued to check him over as if looking for something. I sensed that she was trying to discover the cause of his death. When she found a large wound at the back of Norm's head, I could tell that she had found out what she wanted. **Anger**, radiated from her mind. She clearly believed that some other human had killed Norm. I didn't fully understand what she was thinking, but her mind radiated sadness, anger, and an overwhelming desire to find the killer. What surprised me was that, although she was angry, she wasn't thinking about vengeance – she was thinking about justice.

Justice! That was the word I'd been looking for. The Elder had told us stories to illustrate the human concept of justice, and the special class of ancient warriors that were seekers of justice. These special warriors were often aided by their wolf siblings. Now I began to perceive Alex's destiny ... and maybe mine too. We could be seekers of justice and protectors of the weak, like the special warrior-wolf teams of the long past.

What a thought...

On the next rising of the sun, I went with Alex as she met with *various humans in different structures. Along the way, we stopped at Norm's home, which was previously mine as well. Alex spent quite a bit of time searching around Norm's home and seemed to find several things that interested her. I could tell that she still had a lot of questions in her mind.*

Some of the other sled-pulling dogs had returned, and I visited with them while Alex was busy in Norm's home. When she emerged, carrying some things that she had found, she stood by her truck with the door open and looked directly at me. I knew what she was thinking: did I want to stay with the other dogs or to continue along with her. That was an interesting question. My former master was dead and I had not been given a new master yet. Did that mean I was free? Did I want to be?

I searched my feelings. I wanted to be with her. I didn't know where it would lead, but there was no doubt in my mind. I felt that my place was with her. I raced over and jumped right in. She didn't say anything, but her mind radiated surprise and pleasure.

We visited more humans that day. Sometimes I was able to go into their structures with her, while other times I had to wait outside. As a result, Alex seemed to learn new things, but I didn't. Except for one thing. Other humans seemed to refer to Alex as a **"Mountie."** *I didn't know what that was although, when the word was used, people seemed to be thinking about justice, and Alex seemed to be thinking about helping others. This matched my impressions during the previous cycle of the sun.*

On the next rising of the sun we visited more humans, the most interesting of which was Ruby. This was the Ruby that had been a friend of Norm's and of our entire pack of sled-pulling dogs. I wasn't allowed into Ruby's place, but by staying near the entrance I was able to follow bits and pieces of their meeting. As Alex and Ruby spoke to each other, I heard Norm's name mentioned often and it seemed that Ruby was talking about her friendship with Norm. Alex seemed mostly to be sympathetic.

Then I heard my name being mentioned several times, and

Ruby seemed to be explaining something about Norm and me. Something Ruby said made Alex's mind jump with a start of excitement and pleasure, and the two of them seemed to reach an agreement about something.

When Alex came out of Ruby's home, her mind was racing so much that I had trouble identifying her thoughts. There was surprise, relief, pleasure, and she was thinking about the future. Then I had it! She was imagining her future, and all of her mental images of her future had me in them with her.

*I wondered whether she had just become my new master, but that's not what was in her mind. In her mind she saw me more as a... **friend**.*

I've already explained that my knowledge of human words was improving with every cycle of the sun, but still very limited, so when a human spoke to me — even a human that I'd come to know fairly well — I would only get fragments of their speech. I would hear them as understandable words separated by a kind of mumbling. It was only by adding the understandable words to the human's mental images that I was able to understand the thoughts that were behind them. So, what I'm going to tell you next contains words that I understand now but did not at the time they were spoken to me. Even then, however, there was no mistaking Alex's meaning.

As she stepped out of Ruby's place she stopped, adopted a serious body position and tone of voice and said:

"Silver, I think this is the beginning of a beautiful friendship!"

Laurie Schramm

6 CHILKOOT AFTERMATH

The U.S. National Park Service had a backcountry ranger station at Sheep Camp, so the Guide leaders decided to take everyone the mile and a half down the trail to Sheep Camp so they could report in and get help. Once they arrived at Sheep Camp, it took a while to find anyone to report to.

The two park rangers had been out surveying the extent of the damage from the rockslide, and they were relieved to see them - but concerned about Lucy. Apparently, there had been no hikers aiming for the summit ahead of them, but another group had been camped behind them at Canyon City. This other group had turned back to Dyea as soon as they'd heard the roar of the rockslide and seen the huge dust clouds, and all of them had made it back safely, without further incident.

The Parks Canada Wardens on the Canadian side were now holding back hikers from crossing the summit until the slope was judged to be safe, and until at least some of the covered trail could be restored. The only outstanding concern had been for the patrol of Girl Guides, which now focused to the case of the one missing Guide, Lucy.

Although the patrol naturally wanted to stay and help search for Lucy, the rangers convinced them that they had done everything that they could, and that it was time to leave the search to the professionals.

Beyond Sheep Camp

It was decided that the leaders would take the patrol back to Skagway and await further developments. Having provided the rangers with a description of Lucy, the Guides set out on the rather disheartening hike back. Although they had risen early, at 06:30, it was now well past noon, meaning that they would have to camp one more night on the way back. As they set out on the trail two thoughts were uppermost in their minds:

"I hope they find Lucy!" and
"I hope she's OK."

Meanwhile, the two park rangers had radioed in a situation report and advised their base that they were going to try to retrace the guides' original escape route in hopes of finding

Lucy. This took the rest of the afternoon so that, by the time they had returned to the backcountry ranger station to report their lack of success, it was too late in the day for anyone to do any further searching.

That evening, the Chief Ranger decided that it was time for a better organized and more comprehensive search and started making calls for help from other agencies in Skagway. All of the local emergency service organizations, including police and fire, immediately committed to sending personnel, as did the Alaska State Troopers. Parks Canada had immediately volunteered some Canadian park wardens but, being on the other side of the now-blocked Chilkoot Pass, they would be delayed by having to drive around the mountains to Skagway.

The U.S. Park Service itself had the necessary supporting equipment in storage just outside the Skagway townsite because, sadly, this kind of thing happened all too often in a wilderness park. The local flight-seeing helicopter company immediately agreed to make two of their four helicopters available (the other two were grounded for repairs). Although each would carry a "spotter," their priority task would be to ferry equipment up to Sheep Camp, where the command centre would be established.

The search personnel would meet at dawn the next morning for a briefing, after which everyone would have to hike up the Chilkoot Trail just like everybody else did.

For the rest of the evening all they could do was prepare themselves and wait.

There is a certain amount of excitement involved in participating in a rescue mission, but every one of the searchers-to-be, whether amateur or professional, went to sleep that night thinking some version of:

I hope she's OK.

Laurie Schramm

7 SKAGWAY AND A CALL FOR HELP

The third significant Skagway event occurred on our second day there. While Silver and I were exploring Skagway's downtown area. Having spent most of the morning wandering around the town, I'd been sitting out on the front porch/deck of a coffee shop with Silver when I heard my name called.

"Constable Houston?" said a voice.

Looking up, I saw a medium-sized, middle-aged man that immediately reminded me of James Arness the actor in the popular television series *Gunsmoke.*

"Yes?"

"I'm George Carter, the Chief of Police here in Skagway. I just wanted to meet you and say hello."

"Alex Houston," I replied standing up and offering my hand to shake. "How is it that you know my name?"

"Welcome to small-town America, Alex. Ross and Sally Peake are friends of mine, and they couldn't help talking about the red-haired woman Mountie they'd met and the fact that Silver had become a police dog. They were so proud of Silver, and so pleased to see him again, that I hope you won't mind if they talked a lot more about Silver than they did about you?"

Laughing, I said "Not at all. Would you like to join me in a cup of coffee?"

"Don't mind if I do," George replied, as he took a seat at my table. "Now then, I was pleased to hear about Silver here, but if a woman Mountie is a rarity, then you must be just about the only one that's also a dog handler!"

"Right on both counts," I supplied. "I was kind of a pilot project for the Force, but an entire troop of women Mounties graduated near the end of 1975 plus two more troops of women last year. With nearly a hundred women in the Force I'm not so unique any more, although I'm still the only woman dog handler in the Force… so far, anyway."

For his part, George explained that he'd started out as a U.S. Marine but that after a while he'd wanted a change and had joined the Alaska State Troopers. That also worked out for a period of time, but then he'd switched again – this time to the quieter life of a small-town police chief. That led him into some stories about the challenges of policing a small town that is normally isolated and quiet but that, in tourist season, mushrooms to several times its normal population.

George Carter

"Now we have cruise ships coming in as well. At least two at a time coming in every three or four days!" he'd concluded.

As we continued to chat, I explained how Silver and I had chanced to meet and eventually become friends and partners and that, having learned that he'd been born in Skagway, I'd come to learn more about his origins, which had led to meeting Ross and Sally. I also mentioned that I was thinking of backpacking the Chilkoot Trail with Silver.

George highly recommended hiking the famous Chilkoot Trail, and emphasized that it was best hiked in the same direction as the original prospectors. That is, beginning near Dyea, going up over the pass and into Canada near the summit, and then down to eventually meet the highway. He also warned me that it can be rough going, and to be careful at the higher elevations where, even in the summertime, hypothermia was a serious risk. His advice was to go talk to the park rangers first for advice, and since I'd have to register with them to hike the trail anyway.

After George had taken his leave of us, Silver and I continued strolling around town. The U.S. had just created the Klondike Gold Rush National Historic Park the previous year[14] and they had built a great visitor centre right downtown in the centre of Skagway. The park rangers were extremely friendly and helpful when I explained that I wanted to hike the Chilkoot Trail, and they fussed over Silver a lot – which endeared them to him as well. We left well supplied with advice, trail guides, and topographic maps. The local stores were well prepared for backpacking tourists as well, so we were fully outfitted in next to no time at all.

Notwithstanding my little bit of running around, my first two days in Skagway had been filled with fresh air, beautiful scenery, and wonderful people. It was all so relaxing - especially after our most recent adventures in Nova Scotia[12], and I was starting to daydream about just hanging around and relaxing forever...

I really should have known better than to even think thoughts like that. I was sitting back, relaxing with Silver on the front porch of Ross and Sally's house when a rugged-looking police truck pulled up – it was George.

***

"Hi George," I offered, when he came up to the porch. "Here to see Ross and Sally?"

"No, I'm actually here to see you," he said. That got my antennae twitching.

"What's up?"

"Did you hear about the rockslide up on the Chilkoot Trail yesterday morning?"

"Yes, I did. Ross was just telling me about it. Was anyone hurt?"

"Well, that's kind of the thing. You see there's a young girl missing. Seems a bunch of Girl Scouts were backpacking the trail together when the slide started. The girls were quite a ways down the mountain from the slide, but they were right in line with it so they immediately scattered. When the slide ended and the dust settled, they collected themselves up and found that one of their group was missing."

"Uh oh."

"Uh oh is right. They searched for her but couldn't find her so they eventually went back to a backcountry ranger station and reported in. The rangers there sent them down the rest of the way to town while they went out to search for her themselves. They couldn't find her either."

"What do you think happened?"

"I don't know. She probably ran off somewhere and either had an accident or is just lost in the woods."

"Could she have been caught in the slide itself?" I asked, thinking how horrible that could be.

"It's possible, but according to the rangers, the slide had lost most of its energy by the time it reached the girls, so it would have been more like a dust cloud with some rocks rolling around – nothing that could have covered or buried a person. We think she's out there somewhere, hurt or lost," he paused for a moment of thought, "or both."

I was pretty sure I knew what was coming now. "So, I imagine the rangers conducted a more careful search today?"

"That's right. The Chief Ranger put out a call for help last night. This morning they had two helicopters ferrying supplies up the trail, while a horde of volunteers hiked in to do another search. Between the rangers, police, and fire volunteers they had about as many searchers as they could properly use in that area and they did a careful grid search throughout the whole day and… nothing. That means three failed searches in a row, the two quick and dirty searches made by the leaders and then two of the rangers yesterday, and then the full-out grid-search all day today, and none of them found a damn thing!"

"So, if she's still alive, then she's been out there for a day and a half, and now she'll have a second overnight to deal with. I take it that you're planning one more search tomorrow, and you want Silver and I to come?"

"That's right too. We're worried that time is running out on us. Will you do it?"

Now where had I heard that before?

"Of course we will, but I have to tell you that the odds are not going to be very good."

This prompted Sally, who had been listening through the front-screen door to step out and exclaim: "But I've heard of bloodhounds that can follow a trail after several weeks!"

"I've heard stories like that too, but I really doubt that there is much truth in them. I'm not really an expert on tracking. I can tell you that I have heard some believable stories of police dogs being able to track things after two or three days, but I have an uneasy feeling that that's been under ideal conditions."

"Oh," said Sally, disappointed.

"I just don't want to get anyone's hopes up," I continued. "We won't be searching under ideal conditions. It hasn't rained in the past two days, so that's a blessing. On the other hand, it's not just the time that has passed, we've now had all those hordes of searchers trampling everything down and adding their own scents on top of everything. There's another thing, too… Silver and I have practised tracking people but that's not our specialty. Silver's real training was for explosives."

Sally sighed. "So, it's hopeless then?"

"Oh no, it's not hopeless. Not yet, anyway. We'll go give it a try. Only Silver will know if the girl's scent is still present, so we'll have to trust him on this one. I'm just saying the odds are not good, not good at all." Then, turning back to George, "I'll have to call this in to Ottawa, but we'll do whatever we can to help you." Then, to Sally: "Can I borrow your phone to make a collect call?"

"Of course, but will you be able to get hold of him this late? With the three-hour time-zone difference it will be past midnight in Ottawa."

"I can get a message in any time of the day or night, but there's no telling how long it will take to get an answer back, or what they'll think about it all. I don't know how this cross-border stuff works, but we can count on my boss. He'll either give me an official OK, or he'll know that I'm just going to do it anyway and give me some advice on whether there's a way to do it without getting fired. But just so you know, we're going out with George here no matter what."

"He'll support you," chimed in George, "he won't have any choice."

I just stared at George, knowing there was more to come.

"Didn't I mention it before? She's Canadian!"

"No, you didn't mention that before," I said, looking at him narrowly. "I thought you said they were Girl Scouts?"

"My mistake, they were Canadian Girl Guides. In Alaska we call them Girl Scouts." There was a pause, as George held my gaze for a moment before relenting. "OK, it was a small test."

I raised an eyebrow. "A test?"

He didn't flinch. "Look Alex, I like you, but I don't really know you. Now that things have turned serious, and the going may get tough, I like to know what kind of people I'm dealing with. So yes, a small test."

"Fair enough, I suppose" I said, thinking about it. I wasn't impressed with his 'small test,' but I supposed that he was under stress and worried about who he could count on. I was a stranger, after all, so I decided to let it pass, and simply added: "Let's make the call."

So, I called the phone number that I knew would be constantly monitored, 24 hours per day, and the duty officer in Ottawa carefully took my message to Staff Sergeant Bob Simpson, my boss.

As it happened, I received a call back within fifteen minutes, while George was still there. It was Bob himself.

I briefly explained what had happened, and what I was planning to do. Bob asked a few more questions, gave me some advice, and signed off.

"Permission granted," I said to everyone, "but only if it's clear that I'm volunteering, and George here has to send him a formal request in writing. Since I'll be back on duty, I also have be in uniform."

George reacted instinctively. "Bureaucratic red tape!"

"It's OK," I counseled. "We can count on my boss. Besides, he has his troubles too. He'll have to run this through the Department of External Affairs, and who knows what other departments. If you send in an official-sounding request that will help him. In an emergency, I think they can just grant us the approval and sort out the paperwork later."

"Besides," I concluded, "Silver and I will come with you no matter what they say. If you send the request in by Telex first thing in the morning, you'll get something positive but cautious back from Bob right away. If the bureaucracy gets upset, we'll be out on the trail before anyone can order us to stop – OK?"

"Do you even have your uniform with you?"

"Sure, I always have my tactical uniform in my truck because I never know when we'll be called out on something..." I paused for a moment. "Of course, I don't have my gun with me. I didn't want to bring it across the border, so I left it back in Whitehorse for safekeeping. I'd planned to pick it up again after we leave Alaska."

"That was probably wise. We're pretty relaxed about guns here in Alaska, but it can get sticky at the border crossing. The feds can be a real pain in the ass sometimes…" Then, realizing what he had just said, "No offense."

"None taken, I know what you meant."

"I thought you'd most likely have left your gun on the other side, so I brought you one that I'd like to give you."

I raised my eyebrows at that. "Do you think I need a gun?"

"Probably not, but I'll feel better. Call it a matter of professional courtesy," and with that he reached into a briefcase he'd been carrying and brought out a Smith & Wesson, .357 Magnum-calibre revolver. This was a more powerful revolver than I was used to.

"Do you think I'm going to run up against Soapy Smith[3]?" I joked.

"Not Smith, Alex, bears!"

"Oh, OK," I said, abashed. "Will it stop a bear?"

"Probably not, but it will sure scare the hell out of one! I'm thinking of your dog here, as well. You shouldn't have any trouble in the wilderness with a well-trained dog, but sometimes a dog will go chase a bear, upset it, and then the bear follows the dog right back to its owner. I don't think that's going to happen in your case, but it's possible. Just don't make the mistake of getting caught between a mother bear and her cubs. If you do that, nothing will save you!"

"You're starting to make me think this isn't such a crazy idea after all," I murmured, looking the gun over. Then, looking back up, "You brought this for me, but you also wanted to try your 'small test.' Are you sure about this?"

"Absolutely. I thought I'd read you right when we met yesterday, but I needed to be sure. As far as the gun goes, we just switched out all of our .357 Magnum guns for .44 Magnum – just like in *Dirty Harry*[15] – making the older ones redundant, so I can spare it. Sometime, give one of the new .44 Magnums a try, they can penetrate the door of a truck!"

"OK then… thank you."

"Don't mention it," he said. "One more thing. Gun permits aren't generally required here in Alaska, but some people aren't very keen on foreigners carrying guns here. No offense."

"None taken, I can understand that."

"So, here's what we're going to do, I'm going to issue you a permit, two permits in fact." Then, rummaging through his briefcase, he pulled out two multiple-copy forms that he helped me fill out – one was a gun permit, the other a carry permit. When they were done, he signed them and tore off a copy of each for me to keep.

Just as he was about to leave, George paused and looked at me rather narrowly. "I may be just the small-town police chief you see before you, but I've served in larger organizations too. How is it that a young Constable such as yourself can call Ottawa in what for them is the dead of night, reach a phone number that is staffed around the clock, and then get a call back from your boss within less than an hour?"

"*Uh oh*," my inner voice said. "Just lucky, I guess," I said in what I hoped was an innocent-sounding evasion.

George was clearly no dummy, and he continued to look at me narrowly and let silence be his response.

"Look, I'm not supposed to advertise what branch of the Force I really work for. Can you ask me about it another time?"

"I think you just answered my question anyway," replied George, "but sure, as long as it doesn't interfere with you helping us with the search. Tell me about it some other time."

"Thanks George, I promise." As I said those words, it dawned on me, and not for the first time, that my days of usefulness with the Security Service were surely limited if I kept blabbing my identity all over the place. On the other hand, I needed George to trust me so I'd taken the risk.

After George left, I needed to get some sleep myself and

said good night to Ross and Sally.

"Do you think you'll be able to find her?" asked Sally. She was repeating herself, but we were all worried now.

"Like I said, it's not very likely but we can't just abandon her. We'll just have to do the best we can and hope for the best."

"If she isn't injured, how many days can a person survive without food?"

This was more Ross's area of expertise than mine. "Most people should be able to survive for two weeks without food if they're healthy enough, and if it's not too cold," Ross explained.

"How cold does it get at night up there?" I asked.

"It varies a lot. In these mountains the weather can change quickly from great to terrible. Even now, in summer, we can get anything from wet, cold, and windy conditions, all the way to serious rain or snow storms and whiteouts. Why, I remember a few years ago we had an early fall blizzard snow come and hit us that began with gale-force winds, and ended by dropping five feet of snow on us!"

Sally and I must have looked a bit shell-shocked at this, so Ross relented. "Of course, the weather is actually very good right now," he quickly added. "The low tonight shouldn't be worse than 43 degrees and tomorrow's high is forecast to be 54."

"So, down to six degrees Celsius tonight," I said, mentally converting Ross's Fahrenheit temperatures into metric, "and up to twelve tomorrow."

"What's Celsius?" Ross asked.

"Canada is switching over to the metric system. All our weather reporting changed to metric three years ago, and most Canadians are still struggling with it."

"You don't seem to be having any trouble," Ross observed.

"You can blame that on the fact that I majored in chemistry in university, and all scientists use the metric system. So, I got a bit of a jump-start, you might say."

"Seems strange to me," Ross supplied. "Anyway, as long as the good weather holds, the big survival concern is going to be water. Your Lucy should be able to survive for two to three days without water, but three days is probably the limit."

"But she's already been out there for a day and a half!" Sally exclaimed.

"That's why we need to find her," I chimed in, and with that cheery thought we all went to bed.

Laurie Schramm

8 LUCY

Lucy was strong-willed and intelligent. Both of these qualities were about to be tested. When the Guide Patrol had heard the rockslide, dropped their backpacks and started running, Lucy had dropped her pack, reached in to grab Max, and then hesitated.

Which way should I run? she wondered.

Although everyone else was running to the right of the trail, it sounded to Lucy like the dust cloud might be moving towards the right as it approached, so she naturally crossed the trail and ran to her left, heading for the trees on that side.

Everything seemed to be happening at once. The patrol leaders had tried to keep all of the girls in sight, and it was just bad luck that each leader had stopped to assist stumbling Guides at the same time, so that when they looked up Lucy had already run in the opposite direction. Seeing no other girls nearby or behind them, they naturally assumed everyone else was out in front and had made it to the forest, and they followed in turn. As the leaders and the bulk of the patrol ran onward, none of them noticed that Lucy was not with them.

Meanwhile, Lucy had tucked Max inside the front of her shirt and run in the opposite direction. Having started in that direction, and seeing that the ground ahead of her sloped upwards towards forest, she reasoned that the combination of trees and elevation gain might save her from the approaching rockslide.

When she reached the forest, she found a game trail that seemed to be heading in more or less the direction that she wanted to go, and she just kept on running for as long as she could hear the roaring sounds. This took her up and over the hill, deep into the forest. Although she didn't realize it at the time, this continued to lead her in a generally southwest direction.

Once deep into the forest, she couldn't hear the avalanche any longer, but assumed (incorrectly) that it was because the forest was dampening out the sound. She kept on running, pausing only now and again to catch her breath and make sure Max was safe. Occasionally she stumbled and fell, sometimes due to tripping over a rock or tree root, but then more often because she was running out of energy. During one such fall Max was thrown out of her shirt, but she'd been able to scoop him up and slip him back in place before he'd had a chance to scamper away.

One game trail led to another, but Lucy didn't really take much note of her surroundings, other than to make sure that there was still a fairly clear direction in which to run. Eventually, she stumbled upon a creek. Without conscious thought she followed the creek for a while, until it suddenly ended. Unsure what to do next, and too tired to do much of anything anyway, Lucy collapsed in a heap at the base of a very large and old-looking balsam fir tree.

She would have been surprised to learn that she had run for four miles.

Now that she was no longer running, and as she slowly caught her breath, Lucy moved Max from inside her shirt to sitting in her lap, and her mind turned to thinking about what to do next.

"Where is everyone?" she asked Max, rhetorically. She tried calling out, and yelling for help, but there was no reply. She hadn't seen or heard anyone since she started running, and she remembered now that she'd seen the others running in the opposite direction.

"Did everyone else run in the opposite direction?" she wondered, continuing to talk to Max. There was no way to know.

"Don't panic, Max" Lucy told both Max and herself. "Be prepared."

Some of her Guide training began to come back to her. Their motto, '*Be Prepared,*' meant to be ready, prepared in skills and knowledge for whatever might come. This remembrance provided some comfort and gave her a way to focus her thoughts. They'd been taught that taking time to stop and think was the best thing to do, so that's what she tried to do now.

Take a deep breath, stay calm, and think, she thought to herself. On previous hiking trips the Guides had been taught to find a safe place to stay put if they get lost.

"OK," she said to Max, "we're lost." That was a scary thought, but she pushed it to the back of her mind.

Looking around, she saw that she had collapsed under quite a nice old tree. It had lost its lower branches so that not only was she sitting on a nice piece of ground with a solid back support, her head was just underneath a very thick layer of large branches. It occurred to her that the tree would nicely protect from rain, should a storm come along.

"This might not be a bad place to stay put, Max."

The second thing they had taught the Guides to do was take stock of their surroundings and their gear. Unfortunately, she had lost her pack, having dropped it like everyone else when the rockslide had started. That was too bad, as her pack had held clothes, snacks, and water.

"Well Max, I like this tree, and there's water in the stream that I followed."

She next discovered that her Guides' lanyard and tie were both still around her neck! The tie was actually a fairly large, square piece of nylon fabric, like a bandanna. *That could be handy*, she thought.

Early in her Guiding years, Lucy had learned how to

weave a Guide's lanyard. These lanyards could be worn comfortably around the neck and were fitted with a key ring, to which they were taught to attach a 'Swiss Army'-type knife, a small compass, and a whistle. Lucy's key ring also had a small waterproof container of matches attached to it. So, she did have some tools after all. That made her feel a bit better.

The woven lanyard was about four feet in length, when untied, and was made of four strands of fabric rope. After untying and unwinding it she had four lengths of rope. By tying three of them together she had 12 feet of rope, which she used as a makeshift leash, tying one end to the cat-harness that Max wore and tying a hand-loop in the other end. That left the fourth length of rope, which she set aside in case she needed it for something else.

Next, there were the tools that had been attached to the lanyard. Looking at the key ring, the orange whistle really stood out.

"That was silly of me, Max" she said, "there I was yelling away and tiring myself out when I should have been blowing my whistle!" She tried that next, blowing the whistle like she had been taught: three sharp blasts, wait a bit, three sharp blasts, wait, repeat...

There was still no response to her whistle-blowing, but she was starting to feel a little more in control of things and went back to thinking her way through her situation.

"OK, I can try the whistle again later," she decided, and went back to thinking about water and food.

She had water – that was good. Was it safe to drink it straight from the stream? She didn't know, but she hoped so. Walking back to the stream she saw that it was a bit silty.

"I wish I still had a cup or my water bottle," she said. She could have used her Guide hat as a cup, but had lost it somewhere. She didn't remember it falling off, but it was certainly gone. Still thinking, she absentmindedly began to untie her waterproof jacket, the arms of which had been used to tie it around her waist back when they'd been getting ready to resume their hike. As she untied the sleeves, she was still thinking about what she could use to hold water when she paused and realized what was in her hands.

"Sleeves!" she exclaimed, and immediately tied a knot in the end of one sleeve, plunged the whole jacket into the stream, and then brought it out being careful to use the tied sleeve as if it were a long, narrow pot. *Voilà*, she thought, *a makeshift pot full of water.* Lucy decided she'd have to risk the quality of the silty water, but she wasn't sure about the silt. Dumping the water out she refilled the sleeve, but this time she covered the open end with her fabric tie-bandanna. This made it slow and trickier to fill, but she found that it did a good job of filtering-out most of the silt from the water. With her sleeve full of filtered water, she carefully took a long refreshing drink. That felt much better, and she held the water-filled sleeve out for Max to drink as well.

Her confidence growing, Lucy went back to thinking: *OK now, what about food?* She did have some food for Max. She had stuffed a package of cat treats into one of the breast-pockets of her uniform shirt and, taking it out, she shook out a single treat for Max to eat.

"We'll have to conserve your food I'm afraid," she said to Max.

"Now, what about me?" she mused. Looking around, she didn't see anything encouraging. She thought she had read somewhere that you can eat dandelions, but there were none around this late in the year. *Bears eat berries*, she thought, but she didn't see any berries either.

She knew not to try eating mushrooms, but she had no idea how to decide what plants might be safe to eat. She'd heard that a person could eat some kinds of bugs, but she didn't know which, and the idea of trying any made her feel faintly nauseous.

No bugs then, she thought. *What else?*

Looking back at the stream, she wondered about fish. She wasn't sure if she could catch a fish. There were minnows in the stream but she wasn't sure they'd be safe to eat. *I might try that though*, she thought, *if I get desperate enough.*

"What next, Max?" she wondered out loud. "Shelter and fire."

The fir tree would be her shelter, and she had matches so she could make a fire. Although she hoped someone would find her soon, Lucy decided that building a fire pit would help occupy her mind, so walking back to her tree she started collecting rocks to make a fire circle just in front of where she had previously been sitting. Finding suitable rocks was easy, as everywhere she'd been since the previous day seemed to be covered in rocks of various sizes.

Having built a nice-looking fire circle, Lucy tried a couple more series of blasts on her whistle, and then went to work collecting firewood. On family camping trips her parents had shown her the trick of looking for dead branches on trees, which were guaranteed to be nice and dry, and which could be easily broken off. Soon, she had an impressive-looking pile of kindling.

For her main fuel, Lucy wandered a bit – but not too far from her new campsite – picking up larger branches that had fallen from trees. Max didn't appreciate being on a leash, but he was surprisingly cooperative and behaved himself quite well, she thought.

There were lots of fallen branches, and Lucy soon had a big pile of larger-sized firewood. Some of the larger, and longer branches she dragged back to her tree, where she stacked them to make two rough walls. They actually looked quite nice, although the gaps between the branches were easily as large, if not larger, than the diameters of the branches themselves. "Those walls aren't going to block a lot of wind, Max" she said, "but maybe they'll at least reflect some heat from the fire."

As she and Max scouted the area looking for firewood, she kept an eye out for anything else that might be useful – like an old tin can she could heat water in, but without success. "Oh well," she said, "at least I can have water, fire, and a bit of shelter."

With her stockpiles of wood in place, Lucy decided she

was worn out and, as she kneeled down by her fire circle, she noticed that the light was beginning to fade.

"Just in time, Max," she said. "It will be getting dark soon. I'm glad we started collecting wood when we did."

Lucy tried some more blasts on her whistle, but with no better success than earlier. With a loud sigh of resignation, she tied Max's leash to a low-hanging tree branch and set about trying to build a fire. This, at least, she knew how to do and she confidently set about selecting the tiniest of twigs and branches to use as tinder, then added layers of slightly larger branches, making loose log-cabin-style boxes of them in ever increasing sizes. Selecting some medium-sized branches, she laid these beside her to use in constructing a teepee-shape over the boxes, but later, once the first was started.

Next, it was time for the big moment and she carefully opened her container of matches and took one out. Holding the match so its head was pointing at the roughened surface along the side of the match holder, she gave the match a vigorous swipe.

"*Snap!*" the match promptly broke, right near the head.

"Rats," she said, and she took out another match and tried it again.

"*Snap*" went the next match, as it too broke without igniting.

"Arrgh," said Lucy, disgusted, and all too aware that a container of matches wasn't going to help if she broke them all.

"I know how to do this," Lucy said to Max.

Think, she said, to herself.

"Ok, Max" she said, "the broken matches will now be tinder," and she placed the broken matches inside her little box of kindling. Next, she took a few calming breaths and selected another match. This time, she held the match right next to its head – willing to risk burning her fingers if only she could get the match to light.

She was right on both counts. The match ignited and started to burn her fingertips. Easing her fingers back just a bit, she held the burning match down beside the broken matches and her kindling, and the two broken match heads immediately ignited as well, followed by a wisp of smoke from the smallest of her twigs of kindling.

"It's not lit yet, Max" she reminded both herself and Max, and she bent low and directed little puffs of breath at the smoking twig and burning match pieces. Trying to find the balance between feeding the glowing bits and extinguishing them, Lucy kept on giving cautious little puffs of air. Just when she thought she'd put the fire out, one of the larger twigs caught fire, then another, and then another. Soon, she had a small but distinct fire burning, smoke was rising, and the occasional little "crack" from the wood could be heard. Continuing to blow on the fire, but a bit harder now, Lucy started feeding more small twigs into the fire until it was clear that the next larger-sized branches were going to ignite as well. When they did, she built her teepee of medium-sized branches over the fire, and sat back to watch the fire grow.

Lucy knew better than to build a huge fire that would be hard to maintain and might get out of control, so she kept it to what she felt was a modest, manageable size, but it was still a warming and comforting fire, and she smiled for the first time since the rockslide.

Lucy's smile faded as it once again occurred to her that she and Max might have to spend the night in her little campsite. Her makeshift shelter looked nice, with what she now thought of as 'their' tree and the two walls – more like fences really – that she had built.

"That's not going to be very comfortable," she said. Looking at her lanyard again, it was her knife that caught her attention this time, and she promptly got up and started cutting green branches. This time she selected the longest branches that she could cut with her little knife and, carrying them back to her shelter, used them to fill in the gaps in her shelter's walls, and to make a bed. This turned out to be a lot of work as well, especially since she had to keep building the fire at intervals as well, but eventually she had a thick bed of green branches she could lie on.

Trying out the bed, her first discovery was that it was NOT comfortable. "Oh well," she said, "at least it will keep us off the ground."

As the light continued to fade, Lucy went back to the stream to give Max and herself another drink of water, then spread her jacket out, on a teepee of longish branches, near the fire to dry out. She was going to need that to stay warm at night. The temperature was dropping rapidly now. It was going to be another cold night, but with no sleeping bag or foam mattress this time! Thinking these thoughts, Lucy was suddenly extra grateful for the fire, whose flames rather cheerfully danced in front of her.

Sitting down on her bed of green branches, she watched the evening sky begin to materialize, thinking, and feeding the odd branch into her fire. Now she had too much time to think, and her mind turned to animals. She knew that most animals wouldn't approach her, especially with a fire burning, but it was hard not to worry about them all the same – especially when, from time to time, she'd hear the odd strange noise coming from somewhere out in the forest.

"Sigh," she said, out loud. "I wonder where the others are. I hope they're all OK."

After a while, she put on her jacket – which had been dried by the fire – and stretched out on her bed of branches to try to sleep. By this time, Lucy was so tired that neither hunger nor the strange surroundings could keep her awake, and she fell into a deep sleep, with Max curled up beside her.

***

The next day was the hardest.

Lucy knew she should stay put and wait to be rescued. The park rangers would surely be searching by now, but as the hours went by, it was just her and her tree, and the stream, and the forest.

If breakfast-time without food was hard, lunch-time with

no food was even harder, and by dinner-time a slight stomach-ache had developed into a full-fledged pain in her stomach. She did her best to ignore her hunger though, and spent her time collecting more wood, keeping her fire going, and blowing three blasts on her whistle every now and again. *It is very discouraging*, she thought, *that there is never any reply.*

Where is everybody?

With lots of time on her hands, Lucy also made several forays out to find and cut more green, leafy branches in hopes of building a slightly less uncomfortable bed than she'd suffered on the night before. It was late in the afternoon, when she had dragged her latest batch of branches back to her shelter and she'd thought to use some of them to try to build a reflector wall on the other side of the fire from her shelter. She hoped this would reflect a bit of heat into her shelter at night. Finally, she decided to use the smaller green branches, she had collected, to plug more of the gaps in her shelter's walls. It was while working at this that she noticed a small cairn of rocks near her tree and just outside of one of the walls.

"That's funny," she said to Max and herself, "I don't remember noticing that when we built this wall yesterday. I must have been too busy to look around."

Cairns, she remembered from stories that she'd read, had been used for generations as trail markers and/or as markers of supply caches.

"It can't be a trail marker, Max" she reasoned, "who would put a trail marker in the middle of a forest? Someone must have buried something here!"

Lucy had a sudden fear that the cairn might be some kind of grave marker, but it was so close to the tree that she decided to risk having a look and she moved the rocks to one side. Then, using one of her larger firewood branches as a shovel, she started to dig. It was more like scraping a pit than digging but, again, having lots of time and nothing better to do she continued to scrape away at the soil.

Some of the soil was too hard-packed to move, but there was an oval-shaped area where it wasn't so hard to dig – that suggested to her that something might really be buried there. As she worked away on that area, a small pit began to take shape.

The next issue, was that she had no idea how deep she should dig. Having to scrape the soil out with a branch meant that it took a lot of scraping, and a lot of time and effort for each inch of soil that she got out. However, her persistence was rewarded when, after only digging down about two inches, she struck something.

"This is exciting!" she explained to Max and herself, forgetting for the moment her aching stomach.

Working carefully now, she continued to scrape until she had exposed what looked like the top of some kind of canvas satchel or duffel bag. It wasn't very large on top, less than a foot wide and perhaps a foot and a half long, and her scraping exposed the top of a canvas strap on one side. Digging around the strap, she tried inserting her fingers under the strap and tried pulling it up.

The strap, of course, promptly broke.

"OK, that wasn't very smart," she admonished herself, "I guess it's back to digging."

The bag had a flap with buttons, rather than a zipper, on its top so this time she tried digging all around the bag until she had exposed the whole top, and tried undoing the buttons.

That worked, but not in the way she'd intended. The canvas bag was, if anything, more fragile than the strap had been. The buttons gave way easily for the simple reason that the fabric tore at each button point. Tugging on each button in turn allowed her to easily open the bag along its entire length.

Eagerly, Lucy removed the top item: a fragile looking pouch that looked rather like a large, leather envelope. A leather string held a fold-over flap in place. She couldn't untie the string, but her knife took care of that. Opening the pouch, she found a thin sheaf of folded papers. They were faded, and looked very fragile, but she was able to very carefully open them up.

"They look like letters!" exclaimed Lucy. Holding the pile up in the late afternoon sunlight, Lucy found that she could just make out some of the faded, spidery writing. The top one was a letter addressed to a "Corporal Frank Pool, North West Mounted Police."

"Wow, what a find Max!" Lucy said. "North West Mounted Police, the RCMP hasn't been called that for years. I wonder how old these are."

Peering closely, she could just make out the date on the top letter. It read "February 1, 1898."

"1898!" she exclaimed. "These letters are 79 years old! I suppose this whole case must be too." Setting the pouch of letters aside, Lucy went back to the buried bag and found that the next item was again leathery-feeling, but this one seemed to fill the rest of the bag. She took it out, set it aside, and reached back in to feel around the bag. All she could feel was a smooth, hard surface covered in what again felt like leather.

"Must be the bottom of the bag," she concluded.

Turning to the item she had set aside; she saw that it was another leather pouch tied shut with leather cord. She couldn't untie this one either, so she cut the cord and opened the pouch. Inside was a block of something she didn't recognize. It felt waxy, was greyish-brown in colour, and it looked grainy. The first thing that came to her mind was that it looked like someone had compressed a huge brownie, or a large piece of meatloaf.

"I wonder why the first things I thought of were food?" she asked Max. At this her stomach immediately gave a sharp pang and she groaned out loud. "Because I'm hungry," she answered.

Looking at it the block more closely, she could see that one edge was bevelled. It looked like someone had cut a piece away for some reason.

The next thing Lucy tried was sniffing at it. It smelled like meat that was starting to go bad.

"Meat!" Lucy's stomach gave another sharp pang. This time it was more like the stomach cramps she'd once gotten from playing soccer right after having eaten dinner. Her brain now switched into high gear.

"An early Mountie, travelling from the Yukon to Alaska a long time ago would have had to carry some kind of food. They didn't have freeze-dried food in those days, so it would have had to be something else," she reasoned.

"OK, Max, so what did they carry for food in those days?" Lucy wracked her brain. They had learned about something about this in school, but it didn't have anything to do with police, it had to do with… what? she thought, while turning the waxy block over and over in her hands. Then, suddenly she sat up straight, her eyes wide open.

"Pemmican!" the early English and German settlers in Canada's prairies had learned about pemmican from the Blackfoot Confederacy, Cree, Ojibwa, and the Sioux. She remembered now. She had done an essay on the original plains-peoples for her history class, and had gotten an 'A' on it.

Could this be pemmican? she wondered. That could explain why a piece, or pieces, had been cut away. Her stomach gave another wrenching cramp. Lucy had been without food for a day and a half now, and she'd fed Max all of his cat treats by now too. The water they'd been drinking had not caused either of them any troubles, yet, but she sure was hungry, and she imagined that Max must be too.

Am I hungry enough to try this? she asked herself.

Her stomach said *Yes!*

Her brain wasn't so sure.

She used her knife to cut a thick slice. It cut quite easily. *It's like cutting a soft candle*, she thought. She sniffed at the freshly cut surface. It still smelled like meat that was on the edge of going bad, but it smelled even more like food now.

Wrench! her stomach agreed!

Cautiously, Lucy tried nibbling at the slice that she had cut away from the block. It tasted like, what? "Kind of like a waxy, dried, meatloaf taste, Max" she concluded. She took a few more nibbles.

Needs salt! she said to herself, then started giggling, then admonished herself. *Here I am starving. I find the first thing I might be able to eat, and now I'm being picky about the taste! Some Girl Guide I am.* Suitably chastised, she used her knife to cut another slice, which she instantly devoured. Finding that she could eat it, whatever it was, she next decided to limit her intake to those first two slices.

If I feel OK in the morning then I'll eat some more of this, she decided.

Next, she cut some thin slices and set them out in front of Max. Sniffing them carefully, Max seemed unimpressed as well. *He probably doesn't like the smell of it either,* thought Lucy.

"Come on Max, give some a try," she encouraged. "It tastes better than it smells!"

Max looked up at her and then, whether it was because of her encouragement or his own nagging hunger, or both, he took a small bite. Finding that the taste itself was acceptable, he then gobbled down the rest in a flash.

Feeling somewhat better for both of them now, Lucy went back to stoking her fire, and then set about collecting more dead branches so she'd have enough fuel to see her through the night.

As darkness began to fall at the end of their second day in the woods, she wondered whether anyone was ever going to come and find them, and whether they were going to survive.

The next morning, Lucy got up and looked around. Although she'd tried to wake up from time to time to tend the fire, her tired body had betrayed her and insisted that she sleep. Although she now felt a bit better, their fire had gone out.

"Oh well," she said to Max, "We'll just re-light the fire later in the afternoon instead of wasting any more matches and firewood on it right now."

By way of aches and pains, her stomach informed her that it was still very hungry. The pemmican (at least she hoped it was pemmican) hadn't made either Max or her sick, so she decided it was safe to eat and cut off several fresh slices for each of them for breakfast. It still didn't taste very good, but it was kind of satisfying and she began to feel a bit better.

Max, now that he was used to the taste, had no such reservations. He gobbled his share immediately, and then settled back to lick his paws free of any last lingering traces.

"I wonder what my parents are doing right now, Max, and if they even know what's happened to me," she said. She would have been surprised to learn that her parents had been contacted by leader Brown Owl the previous afternoon, and were at that very moment, boarding a plane to fly to Skagway, via Juneau.

Thinking of her parents brought Lucy a pang of homesickness, but then another thought caused her to lift her chin a bit higher.

"Wouldn't they be surprised to see their little Lucy now, with my shelter, and my water and food, and my... not panicking!"

Later in afternoon, with her firewood re-stocked and more branches added to bolster the walls of her shelter, she decided to take Max for a walk along the stream and explore. A short distance along the way, she found a spot where the stream opened up a bit, and looked like it might be fairly deep in the centre.

"I wonder if there are fish in there?" she said, and she took a few steps out into the stream so she could peer into the deeper water.

She was just considering whether she had any way of trying to catch a fish when there was a rustle in the bushes across the stream, and a little black bear cub walked right up to the other edge of the stream.

What a cute little bear cub, she thought. Lucy watched it intently for a moment and then years of advice about bears in the mountains suddenly flooded into her mind.

Where is the mother?

It's mother probably wasn't too far away, she reasoned, looking to the left and then to the right. She certainly didn't see any other bears... then there was a crashing sound from the forest and she heard a mighty roar.

Lucy screamed.

Max fled.

9 THE THIRD SEARCH

In the morning of our third day in Skagway, I'd wanted to begin by meeting the Guides to see what we could learn from them. The Guide Leaders and Guides had returned to Skagway at around mid-day the day before, which was the day after the rockslide, and were staying at a local motel. George had agreed to meet me there.

Overnight, everyone's worries had magnified, of course, so our meeting was a bit sombre – although the girls clearly enjoyed meeting Silver. Nevertheless, it was interesting to meet leader Brown Owl and the rest, and to hear their story first-hand. The two leaders had contacted all of the girls' parents (back in Alberta), some of whom were flying in later that day. For their part, the girls all wanted to stay in Skagway until Lucy was found, and the whole patrol had decided to stay for at least another day or two. The most vocal of the girls turned out to be Lucy's best friend, Allison Smith, who had apparently been almost frantic ever since realizing that Lucy was no longer with them after the rockslide.

I got a good description of Lucy from Allison and the others, and asked whether they had any of her clothes I could borrow to give Silver her scent. This produced blank stares at first, until Allison piped up: "Hey, wait a minute, we found her backpack, remember?"

Allison immediately dashed off and soon returned with Lucy's heavy-looking backpack. Opening it up I searched through it, looking for clothes that looked recently worn, as opposed to freshly laundered, and I settled on a tee-shirt and a light, fleecy pullover. Allison said that Lucy had worn the tee-shirt for the entire day before the rockslide, and the pullover when she'd been sitting around camp in the previous evenings. I said that I'd like to borrow both for the search.

"You'll be able to find Lucy, won't you?" asked Allison, in a pleading tone.

"Silver and I will both do our very best. I'm sure she's fine, and that we'll find her soon," I said, trying to sound as confident as I could, despite the lump in my throat.

"She's been lost a long time already though, and she's all alone out there…"

"Well, we'll just have to keep our hopes up," I responded. "Sometimes people don't know what they're capable of until they're really tested. She's probably just fine, sitting somewhere waiting for us to find her."

With that, there really wasn't much more to say, and George, Silver, and I drove to the trail-head at Dyea.

The first five miles of the Chilkoot Trail follow an old wagon road. Normally, vehicles were banned from the trail, but in our case, we were able to travel in four-wheel-drive Jeeps. This part was very pleasant. Breathing-in the moist, early morning air, we passed through meadows and forest, and crisscrossed shallow sections of the Dyea River. The forest too, was interesting with its unusual (for me) mixture of trees: birches, spruces, willows, and cottonwoods. Five miles in, the wagon road came to an end at Finnegan's Point and we continued forward by foot, on the trail proper.

As we walked along, it began to feel like real hiking as we followed a three-mile stretch along the river into a narrow canyon for that took us past Canyon City. The first part of the trail followed the river so closely that it had to be forded quite a few times. It was shallow enough at such places that I could pick my way across by stepping on protruding rocks, and in that way, I was able to keep my boots reasonably dry. Silver, however, had to cross in the water each time, leaving him wet, muddy, and probably a bit chilled.

After this the trail started to gain elevation, and I was immediately glad that we only carried medium-sized daypacks, rather than the fifty or sixty-pound packs that a backpacker would have had to carry – or the hundred-pound packs that the original prospectors shouldered in the gold rush days. Three miles of this took us to Pleasant Camp, and then after two more miles we finally exited the forest fringe and into the open (and windy!) part of the trail. This was at Mile 13: Sheep Camp.

At Sheep Camp, standing in an open, rock-covered basin, we were able to take in the stunning views of the ring of mountains that surrounded us. It was beautiful. We had a clear morning, and the sun was reflected by the many glaciers that hung like curtains from the peaks of the mountains that encircled us. I felt that the mountains had a way of looking beautiful and dangerous, all at the same time. The summit was now only four miles away, but a long, long way up. I was suddenly glad we weren't going to make the ascent, at least not that day.

Here also, were the many reminders of why we had come. In addition to the backcountry ranger station, Sheep Camp was where the park rangers had set-up their base of operations for the search. The helicopters had ferried up large prospector-type tents, including several that were clearly kitchen, dining, and storage tents. There was quite a large contingent of searchers, wearing a variety of uniforms, bustling about everywhere. It appeared that another grid-search was about to be launched.

George took Silver and I over to meet Mark Johnston, the SAR[16] coordinator, who was standing over a picnic table that was covered in maps. Mark seemed quite cranky and distracted, although to be fair, he was probably frustrated and worried by their lack of success so far. When I asked if he could assign someone to show me the trails that the escaping

Guides had followed, he initially bristled and I thought for a moment that he was going to refuse. He caught himself, however, just long enough for me to hurriedly explain that if I could go out ahead of the searchers, it would give Silver a better chance of catching Lucy's scent. Mark was able to see the sense in that, so he calmed down and called over two young rangers.

The two rangers were introduced as the ones that the Guides had first encountered after recovering from the rock slide, and who had done the first, hasty search, two days earlier. They were eager to see Silver and I at work, and happy to show us where to start. After giving Silver time to sniff away at the pieces of Lucy's clothing that I'd brought along, he started out and the three of us followed. Silver did his usual thing, darting around here and there, pausing every now and again for some deep sniffing of the ground, plants and shrubs, but it was obvious to me that he wasn't detecting anything related to Lucy.

With the assistance of the rangers, Silver and I tried each of the four game trails thought to have been travelled by the escaping Guides and their leaders. We took our time, and I gave Silver his lead, except when we needed the rangers to start us off on a new trail. It took hours and it was incredibly frustrating, because Silver found no trace of Lucy whatsoever, not anywhere.

Eventually, we decided to return to base and as we did, we passed the main search force, which in the meantime had re-started the grid-search from the previous day. When we reported-in to George and Mark, who were still standing by the improvised map table, they wanted to know what was wrong.

"I really don't know," I'd answered. "Silver has searched everywhere around the trails your rangers showed us, and a few other spots as well, but he hasn't picked up a single trace of Lucy's scent. It's possible that there wasn't much scent to begin with, or that what there was has been masked by other scents by now."

"Are you sure you're any good at this?" Mark had asked.

That was offensive, and I instinctively bristled and became defensive.

"Look, we're doing our best, but Silver can't track a scent that isn't there. Sometimes people don't leave much to follow, and sometimes – I motioned vaguely in the direction of the searchers – the scent gets masked by other scents."

I would have gone on, but George interjected at this point. "Mark, give her a break, she volunteered to come help us and she's doing her best."

"Thanks George," I said, gratefully.

Mark relented a bit. "OK, I apologize, but time's running short and things are about to get worse around here. There's bad weather blowing in from the coast. It's going to be overcast, rainy, and cold by late afternoon. If we don't find her by then, she's likely to get very wet and cold, and hypothermia's going to be a major concern. We can't afford to waste time."

"Look," I said, "I've been thinking about this as we walked back here. Is there any chance at all that we've been searching in the wrong direction?"

That brought Mark all the way back up to a boil. "Look, Missy, I talked to every one of the leaders and girls that were up here and they are all adamant that they ran where we've been searching. We didn't find any trace of the missing girl yesterday, but we were looking in the right place, so now we're going to do it all again."

"Fine, but what if Lucy didn't run the same way as the others? I'd like to try a few other directions, just in case. If she went back down the main trail, she should have reached the ranger station, but what if she ran in another direction? Who knows?"

This just made Mark angry again, of course, but once again George jumped in.

"Let her go Mark. We asked for her help, let's let her do it her way, OK?" George encouraged. "It can't hurt."

"Whatever! Bringing you two in was a waste of time

anyway," stormed Mark.

"Bark!!"

We were interrupted at that point by Silver. While I was arguing with Mark, I'd left Silver off-leash, and had been watching him from the corner of my eye. He'd been wandering around the trail and campsite, pausing occasionally to sniff and look around. Eventually, he'd circled one particular area, given it a second careful sniff, and then promptly sat down and signaled to me with a sharp bark.

He was sitting on the other side of the trail and debris pile! That meant that the rangers and other searchers had been searching the wrong area.

Trying for once to be diplomatic, I turned to Mark and said, "I think we may have been searching in the wrong direction."

He disagreed, of course, calling me "Missy" when he really did know my name, and using colourful language that I'd just as soon not repeat. The gist of his remarks was that he wasn't going to let some "stupid dog and a girl," or perhaps it was "some stupid girl and a dog," distract a professional search.

"Fine, then," I said. "You go your way and I'll go mine. I have just one request: could you spare one person to go with me and make sure I don't get lost too?"

"Mark…" George warned.

"All right. All right. Anything to get you out of my hair," replied Mark, exasperated. Then he straightened up and looked at someone that was behind me and yelled out in a parade-ground roar, "Sawyer! Get your butt over here… Now!"

'Sawyer' turned out to be Julie Sawyer, a Seasonal Park Ranger, working in the park for the summer. Julie appeared to be in her early twenties, was slender but not willowy, had a sparkle in her blue eyes, and a blond ponytail sticking out of the back of her National Park Service Cap. She seemed very alive and energetic as she jogged over to where we were standing.

"You called?" she said.

"I want you to babysit this woman and her dog. Make sure they don't get lost too - and keep them out of my hair!" With that he stormed off.

"He's usually not that bad," explained George, "but he's seriously worried about his lack of success in finding Lucy."

"Well, thanks for backing me up with him. I appreciate it," I replied.

"No problem Alex... To tell you the truth, I actually think that you're wrong about searching that way, but there's one thing I am sure of."

"What's that?"

"I asked for your help, and you should be able to do it your own way. Good luck!" and with that, he shook my hand and walked back to help Mark coordinate the grid-search.

Turning to Julie, I apologized for her getting stuck babysitting us, but she surprised me.

"Are you kidding?" she exclaimed. "I want to do something useful, around here, but someone put an MCP in charge and all I've been allowed to do around here so far is organize coffee and doughnuts!"

"MCP?"

"Male Chauvinist Pig."

"Sounds like he's not your favourite person," I put in. So much for appearances, I thought to myself. Mark was good looking: tall, blond, blue-eyed, and muscular. Odd, I thought, that he and Julie didn't hit it off well, as they were almost stereotypical California beach boy/girl types in appearance. On the other hand, he wasn't my type either, so each to their own.

"Thank god he's not my regular boss or I'd have quit long ago," Julie added with some heat.

I laughed. "OK then, let's go. Come and let me introduce you to Silver."

Silver seemed to take an interest in Julie who, for her part was very excited to meet him. A good beginning, I thought. I brought out the two pieces of Lucy's clothing that I'd brought along, gave Silver a 'refresher' sniff, and told him to track.

He immediately led us off to the southwest, away from the main trail and debris pile, and in completely the opposite direction to that of the organized grid-search. As we approached the forest on that side, I turned my head just in time to see Mark shake his head in obvious disgust and turn away.

Julie had noticed as well. "We're going to hear about this if we don't succeed," she warned.

"Worried?"

"Not me," she returned, with a bright smile. "I'm only a 'useless woman.' Besides that, I'm on the bottom of the totem pole around here. I have nowhere to go but up. So, what do we do?"

"That's the spirit! What we do is we follow Silver wherever he wants to take us. I'll watch him. If you can keep me out of trouble, we'll see what kind of scent he's picked up."

"You really think he's caught the girl's scent?"

"I do. This is kind of hard to explain, but Silver and I have worked for nearly two years now. He knows why we're here, and what we're looking for. If he thinks he's found Lucy's scent, then I really would not bet against him."

Silver, for his part, was clearly 'on the hunt.'

The one common thread in Silver's and my tracking stories is that, while the most intense part is in the tracking itself, when trying to relate the stories later there really isn't that much to tell. Silver would walk in broad, sweeping arcs, sometimes a zig-zag, and sometimes he'd backtrack or circle – always sniffing at everything, the ground, the bushes, the tree trunks, everything. Watching him though, I noticed that in this case his average path always seemed to follow established game trails. That made sense. I assumed that, consciously or not, Lucy would have taken the easiest, fastest way possible to make her escape.

It was slow going for us though, and we'd gone along like this for about three miles, when he stopped for longer than usual on the game trail that we happened to be on at the time.

For a few moments, he just stood there with his head up, looking around. As I came up to him, he looked up at me and I had a sudden impression that he had lost the scent.

Before I could say anything, Silver retreated about five yards, back the way we had come. With his nose so close to the ground I wondered that it didn't fill with dirt, he regained the scent and commenced another zig-zag course, but more slowly this time. Now, the scent led him off the game trail to our right, through the bush and around some large trees. After about ten yards of very difficult slogging through heavy brush, Silver led us back onto the game trail and his pace increased.

"What was all that about?" asked Julie.

"I think he lost the scent, then reacquired it. Something must have scared Lucy off of the trail through the bush, and then she came back to the trail again, I guess."

No sooner had I said this than Julie and I came up against Silver, who had stopped again, but this time with his head down in some long grasses to one side of the game trail. When his head emerged, he immediately sat down.

"Now what?" asked Julie.

"He's found something... What did you find Silver?" I asked, as I walked over to him. Sitting beside one paw was a piece of blue cloth. When I picked it up and opened it up, it was immediately recognizable.

"It's a Girl Guides camp hat!" I exclaimed, "I had one like this when I was in Guides. We're on the right track!"

"We should tell the others," Julie said, excitedly. "Even if we find Lucy, she might need medical help."

"I agree. Do you have a radio?"

"Are you kidding? We just got some of the new Motorolas[17], but they've only been issued to the 'big shots', not the 'little people' like me."

We had a quick conference and ultimately decided to split up. Silver and I would forge ahead and try to find Lucy, while Julie would go back to the search coordination centre and get more help. As we had followed Silver along the game trails,

Julie had been blazing our trail by periodically tying pieces of bright orange flagging tape to tree branches, always at about shoulder height.

The wisdom of this was strongly brought home to me as Julie handed me the roll of tape so I could do the same thing as Silver and I made our way forward. She, in turn, would have no trouble retuning to base or bringing help back, with the way so clearly marked.

"Julie, I'm impressed," I said. "You are way undervalued in the park ranger business."

"All in a day's rangering," she said, brightly. "See you soon," and with that, she set off back to the search base to report in and get more help.

Silver and I continued on with our tracking and blazing. We had another setback when we encountered a shallow stream. It wasn't even shallow, exactly, it was more like a rippling layer of water running along in such a way that it just covered the largest rocks. It was broad though, at least nine feet across. The problem was that as we crossed the stream, Silver lost the scent again. Had Lucy simply crossed the water, like we did, it wouldn't have caused Silver any trouble, as he'd have picked up the scent again on the other side. That didn't happen though.

Lucy must have followed the water in one direction or the other, I thought, as Silver padded around sniffing here and there along the far side of the bubbling waterway. Eventually Silver stopped and looked up at me, as if to say: *"It's gone."*

We were going to have to search along the far side of the waterway, it was just a question of whether to search upstream or downstream. *Fifty-fifty odds*, I thought. "Let's go that way Silver," I said, motioning that we should try upstream.

Silver said "Grruph," and headed upstream. It was a bad choice. It was slow going, as we had to maneuver around bushes and branches everywhere. On the other hand, the bushes were quite thick between the big trees of the forest and the stream, so wherever Lucy exited it seemed like there should be a reasonable scent trail. Eventually, however, I thought we'd gone far enough and Silver and turned around a retraced our steps all the way back to the starting point.

When we reached it, I motioned down-stream, and asked Silver to resume the search. Going in that direction was no easier, so it was slow going, and I have to admit that I was starting to wonder whether we needed to back up again and re-evaluate our strategy.

Finally, after what seemed forever, Silver gave a short "Yip." He had found the scent again, right in front of what looked like another game trail.

"Good Boy, Silver!" I praised. "Let's go find her!"

With another "Grruph," Silver was off. Thankfully, this time the scent was obviously easier to follow, as our pace increased considerably.

We had travelled about another mile when we heard a scream.

Silver immediately barked.

"I hear it too Silver. Let's go, but stay close to me, OK?"

Silver went off in the lead, but stopped at intervals to make sure I was keeping up and hadn't lost track of him.

Silver and I both now had a pretty good idea where Lucy was so we were able to pick up our speed. Any chance of us losing the track vanished when we heard a second scream, but closer now. It was loud! *We're close now*, I thought.

Eventually, we burst into a clearing and saw a girl standing in a stream, facing away from us towards a full-sized, angry-looking black bear.

Silver started to growl.

"Lucy?" I called.

"Yes!" There was a pause. "A little bear cub came along and now her mother thinks I'm a threat."

"Silver. Stay!" I ordered, seeing that Silver was beginning to advance toward the bear.

"OK Lucy. My name's Alex, and this is Silver. We're going to help you... Just stay where you are and stand still, OK?"

"OK, I'll try."

"Where's the cub now?"

"I think it ran back behind its mother somewhere."

"That's good. That's where we want it to be. Hang on a second." If the cub was behind its mother, that was a good thing for us. I certainly didn't want us to find ourselves in between the two bears.

Silver and I moved slowly up to the shore, and there we all were for a moment. The bear, or bears, were on one side of the stream, Silver and I were on the other shore, and dead-centre in the middle of the stream stood Lucy. The moment was soon broken, however. The mother bear, who had been growling and shaking her head and shoulders from side to side, suddenly stood up on her hind legs and gave an almighty, great roar.

At this, Lucy screamed again, and Silver let out another menacing growl. I felt like screaming too, but was focused on the bear.

"Lucy. I want you to try taking a very slow step backwards

110

towards us. OK?"

She was scared but she was brave, and very carefully did what I asked. As she did, I slowly moved to my right while motioning Silver to move to the left.

This seemed to mystify the bear, who went back to shaking her head and shoulders and growling.

"OK Lucy. Try taking one more, slow step backwards towards us." This time, as Lucy took her second step backwards, the bear stopped shaking and swaying and actually advanced on Lucy.

I didn't like the look at this, and my 'spider-sense' shifted from tingling to overdrive. I had previously learned to listen to my 'spider sense' and I did so then.

"Silver. Guard Lucy!" I ordered.

At this, Silver looked at me, then at the water, then back to me again. Then I suddenly understood his quandary. Oh no! I thought, Silver's perennial aversion to going into water wasn't going to help us.

As it turned out, I needn't have worried. After a moment's thought, Silver gave a low growl that sounded exactly like a human groan, and then shrugged and leapt into the stream. In a few bounds he had positioned himself in front of Lucy and started barking at the bear in a ferocious way that would have given any rational human pause. It gave the bear pause too, which gave me the time I needed to take a step into the water – a couple of paces to the right. That gave me a clear line of sight to the bear as I drew the heavy revolver George had given me.

Things were tense now. The bear, having taken one step in the water was shaking its head and growling. Silver was standing protectively in front of Lucy, and growling menacingly. Lucy was standing still, with both hands up and over her mouth, trying to maintain her composure. For my part, I had my gun up and aimed at the bear, and was wondering if I should risk shooting it.

"Lucy. Take one more, slow, step backwards towards shore, OK?"

Lucy was shaking, but bravely said, "I'll try," and took the step.

At this, the bear seemed to instinctively take another step towards us, so I changed my aim and fired two shots in succession at the water, about a foot or two in front of the bear.

The loud sounds of the shots, coupled with the splashes of water right in front of it startled and confused the bear, which halted and reared up on its hind legs again.

"Take another step back," I called over to Lucy.

That next step brought her to the shore, with Silver keeping pace but keeping himself in front of her. I stayed where I was. Lucy was now behind both Silver and I, which was where I wanted her.

The bear seemed thoroughly confused now, and it dropped back down on all four legs to think.

I tried firing one more shot. This time the bullet struck much closer to the bear than I had intended, causing a splash of water that was only about an inch from one paw. That caused the bear to involuntarily take a step backward for the first time, which was just as well because that was going to be my last warning shot. There had only been five rounds in my revolver[18] and I was then down to two. I was going to save those last two in case the bear decided to charge us.

Now time slowed, and for a moment everything went quiet.

Silver had reduced his barking to a low, menacing growl. It was as if he was preparing himself for a very uneven fight, having sensed that the bear was trying to decide what to do next.

The momentary silence was broken by a completely unexpected sound: the long, plaintive whine of the bear cub who, in the woods somewhere behind its mother, was feeling frightened and alone.

That broke the tension. The mother bear had her priorities right: her cub was behind her in the forest, she had an escape route behind her, and we were all over on the far side of the stream. With a very decisive sounding snort, the mother bear simply turned back to the forest and tramped off with her cub.

As I holstered my gun and walked out of the stream, Lucy ran up and threw her arms around me in a big hug.

"Thank you!"

"You're very welcome. I'm glad we found you! Everyone's been very worried – are you hurt at all?"

"No, not really, just wet… and hungry and I've lost Max!"

"Max! Who is Max?"

"Max is my cat. I had him tucked into the front of my shirt but, when the bear scared us, he jumped out and went running off somewhere."

"You brought a cat with you to backpack in Alaska?" I asked, amazed.

"He's my friend. I couldn't leave him behind," said Lucy, as if bringing him along had been the most obvious and logical thing in the world to do. And to her, I supposed, it probably was.

"Max must be terrified. We have to find him!"

"OK, Lucy, we'll go look for him, but first things first. I have some granola bars in my pack," I said, reaching for a couple as I spoke.

While Lucy was munching on the granola bars, I called Silver over and knelt down to give him a great big hug. "Good boy Silver! I can't believe you actually jumped into the water!"

"What do you mean?" asked Lucy, between chews.

"When I called for Silver to protect you, I wasn't sure exactly what he'd do. Silver has a terrible fear of going into the water, especially cold water. On the other hand, he knew he had to get between you and the bear. That meant that he had to overcome his fear of the water in order to be able to jump in and protect you, and I'm very proud of him."

"Can I thank him too?"

"Of course, you can. Come on over."

As Lucy knelt beside me to pet Silver, she had lots of

questions, beginning with whether all of the others from her patrol were OK. When I reassured her that everyone else was safe and sound but worried about her, she moved on to questions about Silver and I.

"How long have you been a Mountie? How many women Mounties are there? How did you and Silver meet, or were you just assigned to each other? ..."

While answering the barrage of questions as best I could, I was watching Lucy carefully. I noticed that she was making short work of my granola bars, while breaking off some bits to feed to Silver. I would not have expected Silver to eat granola, but he did. Maybe our adventure had made him hungry too.

"Have you been starving the whole time?"

"Well, not starving exactly. I had some cat treats for Max, but they got used up. I didn't have anything to eat at first, but then I found something that I think is pemmican and Max and I have been eating that. It isn't very good, though, and I'm still feeling starved."

That was a surprise. "Where in the world did you find pemmican?"

"I'll show you," Lucy volunteered, "but can we please go look for Max now? I'm really worried about him."

"Sure, we can. He probably climbed up a tree somewhere, so he might not be very far away," I answered, trying to sound more confident than I felt. "Do you have anything with you that would have his scent on it?"

"Scent?"

"Right, something that smells like Max, so Silver will know what to look for."

"Can Silver track cats too?" asked Lucy, sounding more encouraged.

"I don't know Lucy, but I hope so."

"Well," said Lucy doubtfully, "Max spent most of his time in my pack, but I lost that when the rocks came flying down the mountain."

"Well, we found your pack and I brought a tee-shirt and a

fleece pullover from it. That's what Silver used to get your scent. It was him that found you here."

"I've been carrying Max around in the front of my shirt. Would that have Max's scent on it too?"

"It will. Kneel down and let's try putting them all together, and we'll see what Silver can do."

Calling Silver to come closer, I pulled Lucy's tee-shirt and a fleece pullover out of my own pack and held them up together, next to the front of Lucy's shirt.

As Silver came over to see what I was holding, I said: "Cat, Silver, track the cat!"

Silver appeared startled, and immediately looked deep into my eyes, as if trying to make sure that he understood what I was asking him to do.

He'd understood me, all right, and I suddenly had the clearest image in my mind of his reaction. If he could speak English, it would have been: *"Me, track a cat? You have got to be kidding me!"*

I suddenly sat down and started laughing.

"What's so funny?" asked Lucy.

"Well, Silver's a terrific tracker, but I seriously doubt that anyone's ever asked him to track a cat before, and I think he's trying to understand why anyone would even want to."

"He understands what we want him to do?"

"Oh, yes."

"And he's questioning your orders?"

"Oh, yes."

"But, aren't you his master?"

"In the human world, yes, I'm his owner and his master. But, in Silver and my special world, he and I are partners and very, very good friends."

I could see that Lucy was clearly trying to get her mind around this, so I tried again. "How about you and Max? He's your cat, right? But are you two master and servant, or are you two very special friends?"

Now Lucy laughed. "Friends, of course. Max hardly ever does what I tell him to do."

"There you go then. Let's just see whether our friend Silver here can help us out." Then looking back into Silver's eyes: "Silver, we need to find Lucy's cat. OK?"

Silver took a long look into my eyes, then gave Lucy a long look, and then I swear he sighed, and stuck his nose into Lucy's clothing and gave each piece the sniffing of a lifetime. He took more time at this than I'd ever seen him do on a tracking hunt before, and at first, I wondered why. Then, I realized that it was because he was working to separate Lucy's scent from Max's.

Eventually, seeming satisfied, he took a step back and began sweeping the area behind us, away from the river.

"How does he know what to do?" asked Lucy.

"I don't know, Lucy. All I can tell you is that he's the smartest dog I've ever met in my life, and he and I communicate so well that I often feel like he can see into my mind. Let's let him do his thing and see what happens."

As we watched, Silver swept a complete arc on our side of the river, then turned around and swept it again, but going in the opposite direction. He'd retraced his steps about three-quarters of the way back before he began to veer off towards the forest, heading for the same game trail that we'd originally walked in on.

"He's found Max's trail," I said. "Now we'll see if he can track it."

With Silver in the lead and Lucy and I following, we headed back the way we had come, but only for perhaps thirty feet, after which Silver abruptly made a sharp turn to the left and pushed his way into the bush where there was no path at all.

We advanced, but slowly. Silver's pace slowed to a crawl as he thoroughly sniffed everything that was low to the ground. It was just as well, because Lucy and I could only make our way with great difficulty due to dense growth of bushes between the trees.

It seemed to take a long time, but we'd probably only gone through another twenty or thirty feet before I heard Silver give out a distinctive snort.

"I think he's found something," I said to Lucy, as I pushed the last couple of branches out of our way before we could see him.

"Where's Max?" asked Lucy.

Silver was sitting beside a very large tree. Sitting exactly the way he'd been taught to sit after finding his quarry in a hunt. The only thing was, we didn't see any sign of a cat.

"Where is it Silver?" I asked.

Silver had been looking at us and panting with his tongue out, giving that wolfy grin he sometimes did. Then, he closed his mouth and meaningfully looked up. Up at the tree.

Lucy and I looked up, and there, on a branch about twenty feet off the ground, was Max.

"Max!" squealed Lucy, delightedly.

"Good boy Silver," I said, going over to pet him, "very well done."

"Come down Max, its safe now" called Lucy, but Max gave no sign of moving. "How do we get him down," asked Lucy, turning to me expectantly.

Now it was my turn to groan: I was going to have to climb that tree and get him.

To add insult to injury, I happened to glance into Silver's eyes at that moment and he gave me a look. It was a look of amusement. I could interpret that look: he'd done his part and actually helped rescue a cat, of all things. The rest, his look said, was going to be up to me.

With a sigh, I removed my hat and pack, and took off my gun-belt. Taking a pair of gloves from my pack, I put them on and started to climb the tree.

It had been more than ten years since I'd climbed a tree, but as a young girl I'd done it quite often. Some of my childhood memories flooded back into my mind as I slowly worked my way higher and higher, all the while trying not to think about falling. When I'd made it up about fifteen feet, there were two stout branches under my feet and I paused to catch my breath and make sure Max hadn't moved. I also looked down and found that both Lucy and Silver had backed up several feet to give themselves a clear view and there they were: Silver sitting on his haunches and Lucy kneeling beside him, with both of her arms wrapped around his neck. Both of them were staring up at me as if I was the day's prime entertainment which, in a way, I supposed that I was.

Fortunately, Max hadn't moved an inch so, with a deep breath, I continued my climb. It wasn't long before I had climbed that final five feet. Now for the tricky part. Max, of course, was sitting far enough out on the branch as to be beyond my reach. The question now, was how far out along the branch I could go before it broke under my weight. The branch was too narrow for crawling, so I stepped out on it, using both hands to hang on to higher branches for support.

Max, for his part, had seen me coming and, although he didn't leave the branch, he did turn around to face me so that he could watch whatever I might be up to. He was watching very intently and, not wanting to spook him, I moved as slowly as I possibly could while trying to talk to him in a soothing voice.

I won't try to relate exactly what I said. It was just baby talk really. The only things I was trying to communicate to him were reassurance and patience. When I got close to him, I tried squatting down so I could get a hand over to him.

He promptly backed up a foot and resettled himself to watch me.

I moved a foot closer. He moved a foot further away.

I judged that I could attempt one more foot out from the trunk of the tree and very slowly did so. Max stood up to back up another foot, but then encountered a problem. He'd moved far enough out that there were no other branches close enough for him to jump to, he was too high off the ground to be willing to jump down, and he'd reached a point on the branch we were on where it split into three very narrow branches. He no sooner stretched a tentative paw further out on one of the narrower branches than it began to wobble dangerously and he sucked the paw back in a flash.

Trapped!

Unsure what to do next, Max said "Meow," and I was just able to grab him by the scruff of the neck before he had time to do anything desperate. I held Max at arm's length for a moment, trying to judge whether he was going to come quietly or come at me with his claws bared. Fortunately, he seemed to judge that he'd had enough excitement for one day and he allowed his body to go limp. Taking that as a sign of surrender, I brought him in and tucked him into my own shirt front.

"You got him!" squealed Lucy, clapping excitedly.

"He seems fine," I said, "we're coming down."

At this point another childhood memory came back to me: trees tended to be easier to climb up than they were down. I'm sure that Max would have seconded that sentiment. Making my way back to the tree trunk was easy. Climbing back down without either falling or squishing Max in my shirt wasn't so easy, but I eventually made it back down to *terra firma* without further incident and extracted Max from my shirt.

While Lucy and Max conducted a joyous but tearful reunion, I put on my gun-belt and pack and received a wave of commiserating licks from Silver.

I'd continued my practice of tying pieces of the colourful flagging tape onto trees as we'd followed Silver into the woods, so it was a simple matter to retrace our steps to the original game trail, and once there I asked Lucy where she'd been sleeping.

"My campsite is near here and I have a fire burning that we should put out before we leave. Besides, we could sit by it for a minute and get warmed up too."

"Sure. Show me the way and I'll keep tying these pieces of flagging tape onto trees as we go so the rangers can find us."

Just like Lucy said, her campsite was close by, near the end of the stream. As we walked there, she described her adventure, including how she had built a makeshift shelter around a big, old tree, and how she'd built a fire circle, and improvised a way to drink water from her jacket.

"You're an impressive young lady!" I exclaimed.

"Wait until you see this," she said, and showed me the packet of letters.

As I carefully opened them up, Lucy attached her makeshift leash to Max and put more wood on the fire.

"These are amazing," I said, leafing through them. Letters to a North West Mounted Policeman, and all dated in the early months of 1898. That means he was here during the Klondike Gold Rush and might have been one of Sam Steele's force."

"Who's Sam Steele?" She asked.

"Probably one of the most famous Mounties ever[2]. He was sent to help maintain law and order on the Canadian side of the pass, but he and his force often travelled down the Chilkoot Trail to get to Skagway and the ships that could take them to Vancouver and connect with the Trans-Canada Railway.

"Now look at this," said Lucy, passing me a leather-wrapped packet. Inside was a block of waxy-looking solid. "Would you like to try some?"

Well, I certainly did not, but she was so eager to share her experience with me that I didn't have the heart to disappoint her. She used her knife to cut a small piece for me and I tried it.

"Tastes kind of waxy and bland," I offered. "I think you're right about it being pemmican though. I tried pemmican once when I was in Saskatchewan. It tasted a bit like this, but with berries in it."

"I wasn't sure if it was food a first," Lucy said, "and then I worried about it being seventy years old, but I was so desperate for food that I decided to try a little bit. Max did too. Then, when I woke up yesterday morning and neither of us was sick, I decided we could eat some more. The two of us have been eating it ever since."

"Well, I've read that really well-made pemmican can last for decades, but I've never heard about it lasting seven decades. I suppose that it had something to do with being well wrapped, buried, and stored in such a cold climate. You were very lucky to find it." Then, looking at the letters again, I asked "Where did you say you found these things?"

"They were in an old canvas case or bag of some kind, buried underneath a cairn of stones, and right beside my tree... Here, I'll show you," she said, getting up from the fire.

Sure enough. In a shallow excavation close to 'her' tree, Lucy had exposed the opened top of a canvas bag or case.

"The bottom feels solid, so I figured that I'd pulled out everything that was in it, and I just left the rest in the ground," she explained.

"That would make it an awfully small bag," I mused, bending down to look more closely and feel around inside. "I wonder if there's more there to see..."

So that's how it came about that George, Julie, two other park rangers, and a paramedic emerged from the forest trail to find a dog and a cat watching Lucy and I use tree branches to dig in the ground near a big, old, balsam fir tree.

"What in the world are you doing?" George asked.

"Anyone got a shovel?" I responded, looking up at them.

One of the rangers actually had a small, collapsible shovel tied to the side of his pack, and we soon had the canvas bag fully exposed, and Lucy and I put our hands in to lift it out.

"It's heavy!" we both said, in unison, as we lifted it out and placed it on the ground in front of us.

"It's an old kit bag," George exclaimed, "and look at the marking on it."

The bag was dirty and faded, but on one side of it we could clearly make out a stenciled symbol – that of capital letter 'P' superimposed on the right-hand side of a capital letter 'M.'

"MP," I said. "This was a North West Mounted Police kit bag... but let's see why it's still so heavy. Lucy, since you found it why don't you see what else is in there."

"OK," she said and, reaching on with both hands, she carefully lifted out yet another leather-wrapped object. This one was about seven inches long, by four inches wide, by two inches tall.

"Lucy, why don't you go ahead and unwrap it for us?" When she did, we all got a surprise.

"Gold!" we all said. It was a solid-looking gold bar.

I hefted it, experimentally, in my hands, then put it back down. "It must weigh close to twenty-five pounds[19]," I said.

George and I looked at each other. "A gold bar in an 1898 Mountie's kit bag would have come from the Klondike," I reasoned.

"It was probably on its way to the Bank of Canada," said George. "They would have brought them down through the pass to Skagway and then by boat to one of the cities along the coast, probably Vancouver, and then caught a train east. I'm going to have to hang onto that bar for a while, so we can see if we can identify it and its proper owner."

"Awww," spoke up Lucy.

"He's right Lucy," I agreed. "I think it's probably Canadian gold, but it's been found on U.S. soil, so the local police have to check it out first. But don't worry, we'll take some pictures of it and George here will give you a receipt for it. If they can discover who actually owns it then I'm sure the owner will pay you some kind of salvage or recovery – right George."

"Right," said George. "Besides, if we can't find the legal owner within ninety days, then we'll give the bar back to you."

"The whole thing?" Lucy exclaimed.

"The whole thing." George confirmed. "After all, you found it, right?"

"Not really," Lucy said, losing some of her excitement, "It was Alex here that suggested we dig the bag out and look inside. I thought it was empty."

"Oh no!" I said, "Thank you for trying to be honest, but you found the cairn, you found the bag, and you found everything that was in it. I only helped you."

George and I exchanged another long look.

"Well, that's that then," said George, with a twinkle in his eye. "Why don't you let me carry it for now, and we'll take some pictures of it and I'll write you a receipt when we're back in town?

The paramedic checked Lucy over and declared her fit for travel. Lucy, however, wouldn't budge until the paramedic had checked Max over too. With a chuckle, the paramedic agreed, checked Max over, and then with a completely serious expression and tone of voice declared Max fit to travel as well.

I flashed a grateful smile at the paramedic, who winked in reply.

Next, we turned to extinguishing Lucy's fire. The rangers were very impressed that she'd built a proper fire circle to help keep her fire contained, and said so.

"We heard shots," said Julie. "What happened?"

"There was a bear!" said Lucy, before I could utter a word. "Two bears, a little cub and its mother, and the mother must have been worried about its cub. Max ran off, and I thought the bear was going to attack me but Alex and Silver jumped in to save me!"

As the others looked my way, I filled in the rest of the story, including the part about firing the warning shots. "Turns out you were right about having the gun George... Thank you," I concluded.

"When you said you were planning to hike the trail alone, it gave me an uncomfortable feeling," George explained. "I'm glad I paid attention to it."

The rangers, for their part had visibly relaxed during this exchange, and I could tell that they were relieved that I hadn't actually shot the bear, and particularly relieved that they weren't going to have to take on the dangerous task of trying to locate a potentially injured bear. I wouldn't have wanted to try that myself.

Eventually, with a last look at Lucy's campsite, it was time to leave. Before we did, I impulsively performed a small ceremony with Lucy.

"Lucy," I said, rather formally, "you did a fantastic job of looking after yourself out here and as one Guide to another, I can tell you that Girl Guides and Girl Scouts everywhere would be proud of you!" Saying that, I extended my left hand and offered her the Guides' handshake.

"Hear, hear," announced Julie, "I was a Girl Scout myself and I couldn't agree more," as she straightened up and offered her the Guides salute.

At this, Silver sat up straight with his eyes shining. George and the other park rangers, for their part, silently stood to attention and saluted her as well. As we all held position for a few moments, it made for a very touching moment – one that I will always cherish.

Then, we headed out with the rangers in the lead and the paramedic walking alongside Lucy, Lucy with Max in her shirt, and George, Silver, and I bringing up the rear.

When the others were far enough ahead of us to be out of earshot, George said, in a low voice, "About the gold. Stretching the truth a bit back there weren't you?"

"What do you mean"" I asked, trying to sound innocent.

George just looked at me.

"OK, well, maybe just a little. But I think she's been through enough, and I'd like to see her get all the credit for the discovery, and if there's a reward at the end of it all, then I'd like to see her get that too."

"Hmmm, hmmm, and the fact that since you're on duty you wouldn't have been able to claim any reward anyway?"

"Just one more reason to do the right thing, wouldn't you say George?"

"I would indeed. I knew you were going to turn out to be one of the good ones. It's been a pleasure to meet you Alex."

"You too George. You too."

We walked the rest of the way back to Sheep Camp in companionable silence.

To cap the day off, Mark, the SAR coordinator, even apologized and thanked me for finding Lucy!

Julie loved seeing that.

Mark's contrition surprised me a bit, at first, because I was sure that he wasn't pleased to have been wrong about Lucy's whereabouts. Thinking about it, though, I suspected that he was smart enough to realize that a successful search looked better for him, and his record, than an unsuccessful one. Anyway, the important things had worked out well, so I let it go.

As a result, everyone was in good humour as we all hiked back to Finnegan's Point, and from there the Jeeps took us back to the trail-head and on to Skagway.

Laurie Schramm

10 DUTY CALLS

News had travelled fast, and there was a crowd of people waiting to meet us at the Dyea trail-head. In addition to the park rangers and other searchers, the Girl Guides and their leaders were conspicuous in their uniforms. Others in the crowd ranged from the parents of many of the Guides, to local citizens and, of course, the media.

At first, all of the attention was on Lucy's reunion with her Guide friends and leaders, with her parents, who had just flown in from Alberta, and with her best friend Allison. Allison, in particular, had been frantic with worry, upset at being separated from Lucy and, of course, horrified at the thought that Lucy might have been injured or killed. Seeing Lucy return relatively unscathed, and with Max intact, had produced relief and whales of tears.

Silver and I were able to meet Lucy's parents, Glen and Vicky, who were naturally very relieved and thankful to have her found and returned safely. I replied with the simple truth: that I was just glad we'd been able to find her. Julie, who was standing nearby didn't let me get away with that, however.

"But it was you!" she interjected. Then, addressing the group of people around us, "Everyone else was searching in the wrong direction. It was Alex that wanted to search another way, but no one would listen to her, so in the end she told off Mark and went her own way! Right George?"

"She sure did!" agreed George, who had been standing at the edge of the crowd, quietly listening. "If Alex here hadn't stood up for her instincts, I'm not sure we would have found Lucy in time."

That sobered everyone up in a hurry, and I hastened to fill the sudden silence.

"It wasn't just me. Silver had found a scent where there shouldn't have been one. It was both of us that wanted to search in another direction... Like always, Silver and I did it together."

That made Silver the centre of attention, and brought everyone back to a celebratory mood. Knowing that he wasn't particularly used to crowds, I thought that Silver was very patient with so many people wanting to come up and pet him. At one point, after this had been going one for a while, he looked up at me with what I thought was a very martyred—looking expression.

Partly to give Silver a break and partly to give Lucy credit, where credit was due, I turned back to her parents. "You should be very proud of Lucy. A lot of people would have panicked and hurt themselves. She had to run from the rock-slide, of course, but she kept her head and controlled her fears, and she was very resourceful. In a very real way, she saved herself out there. Also, you're probably not very pleased with her for smuggling Max along for the trip, but in the end, she saved his life too. If the Guides have a merit badge for lifesaving, I think she more than earned it."

Glen and Vicky were too relieved to have their daughter back, and too proud of her as well, to be upset about the cat.

The celebrations continued for a while, but inevitably the days of stress coupled with the emotions of a successful conclusion brought a wave of exhaustion over everyone and the reunion broke up with the usual thanks, congratulations, and promises to keep in touch in the future.

Ross and Sally had invited George and I to their place for dinner, and both of us gratefully accepted. As we all separated to our respective vehicles and went our various ways, I found myself in a reflective mood. In this adventure, like in my most recent assignment since joining the RCMP, I had experienced more than my fair share of mystery, challenges, danger, and excitement. Along the way, I had once again made some interesting new friends, but friends that I would soon have to leave behind when Silver and I moved on.

Of course, I had no idea at the time how soon that time was going to come.

***

Dinner conversation with Ross, Sally, and George, never strayed too far from our adventure, and at one point I got the opportunity to fill them in on a few loose ends.

"Lucy says she's going to donate those letters she found to the RCMP Museum at Depot Division in Regina. That's good of her," I reflected. "I remember spending quite a bit of time in the museum when I was a recruit in training there. There might be something of historical value in the letters, and I think I'd like to have a look at them myself if I get a chance."

"What about the gold?" Sally asked.

"Well, did you notice that I snuck off to make a phone call at one point?"

"I did," said George, who never seemed to miss much. "I assumed that you were calling your boss to fill him in on the results of our search."

"Ah, well, yes, I probably should have done that," I said, a bit sheepishly. "I'll do that tomorrow, I think… What I actually did was call a banking friend in Radium City[5]. I asked my friend about the gold. He said that if the Bank of Canada's ownership is established, they'll probably pay Lucy a recovery fee of 10 or 15%."

"So…"

"So, he said that in 1898 gold was worth slightly over twenty dollars an ounce, but now it's worth about $170 an ounce."

"And a bar of the stuff?"

"Well, apparently a standard bar, he called it a gold ingot, is worth about seventy thousand dollars."

"Holy smokes!" said Ross, "that means Lucy could get as much as ten thousand dollars!"

I nodded. "Pretty cool, huh. I think she earned it!"

As we were all sharing our surprise and pleasure at Lucy's good fortune, the phone rang, and Sally went off to answer it. When she came back, she had a strange look on her face.

"It's for you Alex. There's an Air Force Captain Harrison calling for you."

"Uh oh," George raised his eyebrows and gave me a knowing look.

"Yes, I think you might be right," I said, getting up to go to the phone. Sure enough, it was Don calling, from somewhere…

"I hear your vacation was short-lived?" Don began.

"How'd you hear about that already?"

"I've been talking to Bob, your boss. He says that you've become an '*International Mountie*.' How did things work out on the search?"

"Everything worked out well. I made some new friends and we were able to save a young girl, but…"

"But what?"

"Nothing, it's just that I'm like the Lone Ranger all over again."

"The what?"

"*The Lone Ranger*. You know, the Texas Ranger and his horse Silver, from fiction, from the movies and television. Anyway, never mind. It's just my own little joke."

There was a pause on the line, as Don thought about what I'd said, then: "I get it!" he said. "You get called into town, save the day, and then while everyone else is celebrating you quietly move on again, just you and your best friend, Silver. Right?"

That was Don, smart, perceptive, and well grounded. No

wonder I'd missed him so much. I sighed contentedly. "You're one in a million, Don, you really are... So, what's so important that you tracked me down?"

"We need your help."

"What's up?"

"I can't tell you on an open phone line. Let's just say that it's not too dangerous, but we really need your and Silver's special talents. It's important enough that my boss called your boss, to make the request, and Bob agreed immediately. That's why I was talking to him and heard about your aborted vacation."

"Ok then. When and where do we meet?"

"Yesterday!"

"What? Seriously, Don, ..."

"Well, right away then. We're sending a chopper to pick you up at the Skagway airport. It should be there in an hour. I won't be on it, but I'll see you soon. OK?"

"OK Don, we'll be there."

After saying goodbye to Don and hanging up, I told George, Ross, and Sally that something had come up and Silver and I were needed somewhere else. I explained that a helicopter would be coming to get us at the airport, and could I leave my truck somewhere for a while?

George gave me that penetrating stare he always seemed to be able to switch on, but his eyes were twinkling. "Things seem to happen around you, don't they? I seem to recall that yesterday you were able to call Ottawa in the middle of the night and not only reach a constantly monitored phone number, but to have your boss call you back within an hour. Now, your government is able to reach out and find you in the middle of nowhere, and there's a helicopter on its way to come get you. Something tells me it's not going to be an everyday civilian helicopter, is it?"

"Probably not," I allowed.

"And this Captain Harrison of yours might not be a real Air Force Captain?"

"Actually, I think he really is," I said, and then I frowned,

"Although he's a bit more than that."

"Hah, I thought so. Do you want to tell me?"

Oh well, in for a penny, I thought.

"I can't say anything more about Don, but everything I told you about Silver and I is true - it's just not the whole truth. As you've probably figured out, I work for the RCMP Security Service and have been for nearly two years now. Having a woman Mountie and a highly unusual-looking police dog working for them was like a double cover, and I guess they couldn't resist taking advantage of it. So, they just send us wherever they need us, whenever they need us. Usually undercover."

"So, you're kind of a female James Bond then?"

I laughed. "I've never really thought about it that way, but if you take away Bond's licence to kill and just focus on criminal matters, then I suppose so. Maybe I should try drinking martinis – shaken, not stirred?"

"Tell you what. Come back for another visit sometime and I'll buy you one."

"Deal."

"And thanks Alex, I really mean that. You and Silver saved a life here today – and save your breath," George rushed on before I could object. "I know you'll tell me that you were just trying to do the right thing, but we'd never have found her alive if it hadn't been for you. Everyone here knows it, and everyone really appreciates it – even Mark!"

He laughed at that. "In fact, it was a good lesson in humility for him. Mark is a better fellow than the one you saw in action, but he still has some growing up to do, and you and Silver just helped him. Thank you for that too."

"Well, you're welcome. I'm just glad it all worked out."

"Come on, I'll drive you to the airport and then I'll put your truck in our police compound where it will be safe until you can come back and pick it up, along with those martinis we're going to have."

So, I went and packed-up, and then thanked Ross and Sally for their hospitality, and for the chance to meet Silver's family too. We had an emotional goodbye, culminating in them making me promise to go back and visit again, with Silver, of course, to which I readily agreed.

***

It wasn't long after George, Silver, and I reached Skagway's airport, that we could hear the heavy '*Thump, Thump, Thump*' sound of a large helicopter approaching. Next, we saw the approaching lights, and finally the unmistakable appearance and blasting roar of a Canadian Forces Sea King[20] helicopter.

"Like I said," observed George, "not your everyday little civilian helicopter."

I just shrugged and grinned.

I had shown George the place in my truck where I stowed my red flashing light with magnetic roof mount base and with that in place, flashing on the roof, George simply drove my truck out onto the tarmac and right over to the helicopter. When we got there, a Lieutenant in a flight suit hopped out to meet us.

"Constable Houston?" he said.

"That's me," I agreed.

"My name's Sandy. Captain Harrison said to look for a fiery woman with red hair, and a grey-white dog that looks like a wolf!"

"I am not a fiery woman!" I instinctively retorted. Then, having listened to what I'd just said, and hearing George burst out laughing, I grinned sheepishly. "Maybe Don knows me better than I know myself," I allowed.

Sandy laughed as well. "Hop in!"

A crewmember took my two duffel bags and a third for Silver. Over the whine of the pilot re-starting his engines, I said goodbye to George and I jumped in, with Silver following close behind me.

The big helicopter took off as soon as the SAR Tech[21] signaled that I was belted-in and that Silver was reasonably secure beside me.

After that, all any of us could hear was:

"Thump, Thump, Thump…"

... Alex and Silver will return,
in *An Inseparable Mountie.*

Laurie Schramm

SUMMARY

RCMP Constable Alexandra Houston finally gets a break from a series of hair-raising assignments and heads for Alaska on vacation. While there she hopes to investigate the origins of Silver, her best friend and police-dog partner, and hike the famous Chilkoot Trail. Meanwhile, a young Girl Guide gets lost in the wilds of Alaska and comes to experience first-hand the meaning of the Guides and Scouts motto: *"Be Prepared."*

Laurie Schramm

ABOUT THE AUTHOR

Laurie Schramm comes from an RCMP family, grew up while living in the RCMP Barracks (Depot Division) in Regina, Saskatchewan, and spent several summers working as a civilian for the RCMP while in high school and university. Early personal influences included not only the real-life RCMP culture but also Hollywood's versions via such classics as Rose Marie, and Susannah of the Mounties. Many of the events described in this novel are based on the author's real life, although not necessarily within an RCMP context.

For more information, see Laurier L. Schramm on **Linked** in

and:

www.laurieschramm.ca

or

www.facebook.com/LaurieSchrammBooks

Laurie Schramm

ENDNOTES

1. Later renamed Royal North West Mounted Police, and later yet the Royal Canadian Mounted Police.
2. Superintendent S.B. (Sam) Steele, was one of the heroes of the Klondike Gold Rush (where he was referred to variously as *Steele of the Mounted*, or the *Lion of the Yukon*), and one of the most famous Mounted Police officers of all time.
3. Jefferson Randolph Smith II, commonly known as *Soapy Smith*, was a notorious confidence artist and gangster-boss in the late 1800s American West, principally in Texas, then in Colorado, and finally in Skagway, Alaska. He was killed in a famous Skagway shoot-out during the 1898 gold rush.
4. Invented by Indigenous Peoples, and a staple of pioneer travelers in Canada's West, pemmican was made from dried, finely pounded bison meat mixed with melted fat and sometimes other ingredients, such as bison bone marrow. Well prepared and stored pemmican has been known to last for more than fifty years.
5. See *An Inconvenient Mountie* (ISBN: 978-1-9994940-0-1).

6. At this point in time, it was still part of the RCMP Years later, in 1984, the Security Service was spun-out to create the present-day Canadian Security Intelligence Service (C.S.I.S.).

7. Although dog teams originally played critical roles in Alaska's and Northern Canada's evolution, snowmobiles (the 'iron dogs') had almost completely replaced them by the 1960s. The 'Iditarod' was conceived as way to celebrate Alaskan history. A first, two-heat, race was held on part of the Iditarod Trail in 1967 and 1969 (there was a lack of snow in 1968). After completion of the entire trail, all the way from Anchorage to Nome, the first full-length *Iditarod Trail Sled Dog Race*® was held in 1973.

8. It wasn't until 1988 that younger girls could join the Guiding movement (at age five), and not until 1989 that they got their own name: 'Sparks.'

9. Inukshuk is derived from an Inuktitut word, and refers to a human-built stone marker (cairn). They are characteristically found in the Arctic, Canada's northern territories, and Alaska.

10. Girl Guide leaders generally adopt fun names, which can vary widely in nature. In this case the girls' leader had advanced from Brownies to Guides with the same group of girls and had, for simplicity, kept the name she had used as a Brownie leader: 'Brown Owl.' (Brownie Leaders traditionally adopt the names of Owls.)

11. In avalanche training, mountaineers are taught that if some of their expedition is caught in an avalanche, then they should first conduct a 'hasty search' in what seems like the most likely location for their colleagues to be buried. If that fails, then they are to re-start the search but this time over a wider area, and with a careful grid-search

methodology – which can be extremely time consuming.

12. See *An Indestructible Mountie* (ISBN: 978-1-9994940-4-9).

13. This chapter, in slightly longer form, has also appeared as the short story "An Inhuman Mountie" on www.laurieschramm.ca, 2019.

14. In June, 1976.

15. *Dirty Harry* was released in 1971, the first in a series of American action/crime movies in which the central character famously carried the powerful .44 Magnum revolver.

16. Search and Rescue.

17. When Motorola launched their MX300 hand-held VHF radios, in 1975, they set a new standard in portability and performance, and the radios were quickly adopted by police, fire, military, and other forces.

18. Although the revolver held six rounds, I was taught to only chamber five, leaving an empty cylinder under the gun's hammer. That way if the gun was ever dropped, it couldn't accidentally fire.

19. It later turned out to be a standard 400-ounce gold bar, 7" x 3⅝" x 1¾", and it weighed exactly 25 lb.

20. Sikorsky CH-124 Sea Kings are twin-engine, anti-submarine warfare helicopters that were used by Canadian Forces for over 50 years. They were usually housed on and deployed from destroyers and frigates of the Royal Canadian Navy. Sea Kings were a familiar sight to people on Canada's Pacific and Atlantic coasts in the 1970s, partly because they frequently assisted with maritime search and rescue operations.

21. Search and Rescue Technician.

Laurie Schramm

ADVENTURES OF THE FIRST WOMAN MOUNTIE

Book 1: *An Inconvenient Mountie*
Book 2: *An Inconspicuous Mountie*
Book 3: *An Indestructible Mountie*
Book 4: *An International Mountie*
Book 5: *An Inseparable Mountie*
Book 6: *An Indispensable Mountie*

www.laurieschramm.ca

www.facebook.com/LaurieSchrammBooks

Laurie Schramm

www.ingramcontent.com/pod-product-compliance
Lightning Source LLC
Chambersburg PA
CBHW032016170626
46807CB00006B/2830